The Secrets of Gelid Lake

V.Mull

Author

V.Mull

Young Adult Fantasy Novelist

Published by Underwater Ally Publishing
Copyright © 2022
All Rights Reserved
ISBN: 979-8-9858061-4-4

Visit Authorvmull.org for more information.

Cover artist: Jessica Dueck - Jessicadueck.com

Thank You!

To my family for their constant words of encouragement, I appreciate it!

To my A15 moms – I know I can count on you for the best support.

To my dear friends, Kali and Kylisha - I wake up every day excited to share with you what shenanigans my characters have gotten into. I love how we can go from subject to subject, all sharing our work with each other and acting as if our characters are alive. You two are the best!

To my editor, Donise – I adore all the hard work you put into my work, the positive comments, and the wonderful suggestions that make me love the books even more.

To my cover artist, Jessica – You never cease to amaze me! This cover was beyond perfect. It was like you read my mind when you created it. And it's wonderful.

Table of Contents

Chapter One
Nathalia of the Trees

I stopped aging three years ago, but no one has noticed. Only the lake sprites and the silver fox know. They call me the Cold One, but I'm not a vampire, and I never died. I just climbed the wrong tree on the wrong night.

I was an adept tree climber and conquered the tallest trees in our town. I'd sneak out with a small lantern at night, avoiding the inevitable confrontation with my mother for doing something so "inappropriate for a lady." It was invigorating to climb so high. I felt powerful atop the branches, like the townspeople and their judgment couldn't reach me.

My laced boots hit the dirt with force as I jumped from the last tree. It was a challenging one, taking me over half an hour to strategically weave in and out of the thinning branches. I walked home considering which tree I should climb next. There was a fat maple in the grove a mile outside of our town. The two walnut trees would be fun to jump between, but they didn't seem difficult enough.

Then the thought came to me: the great, three-hundred-year-old sycamore whose roots dug deep into the soil, while its branches hung dangerously close to Gelid Lake. The lake was absolutely forbidden to all – not one living creature dared swim in it. No matter the season, it was beyond ice cold. One would immediately get frostbite if they touched it. On a clear night, the moon would illuminate it to a haunting, glowing blue hue. It would be the ultimate challenge, standing at over one hundred and fifty feet. So, I made my plans to sneak away after dinner. I'd need ample time to travel the six miles.

I removed my moon and star charts from the little desk in my room.

Full moon, I thought and tapped the desk. I'd have to pack a bag with water and pants. My skirts and petticoat would snag on the branches, and I didn't need extra trials.

"Ma, may I go for a walk to get some fresh air tonight? My headaches are coming back," I said at dinner.

She scoffed, as she usually did when I spoke, like I was constantly interrupting her thoughts. "Fine. Stay within the town lines." She knew how badly I wanted to venture out, and I had low impulse control. I nodded and slid the chair back.

"Nathalia …"

I looked at my mother.

"No trees."

Ma cared too much about what people thought of her, and my climbing trees brought more attention to us than I already received on a daily basis for my "odd behavior." She often mentioned how people would confront her about seeing me in a tree, my dress and stockings constantly tattered from the rough bark and boy did it embarrass her.

"Rein that girl in," Ma said, mimicking the voice of Mrs. Hanson from down the lane one day. "They think you're wild, Nathalia, and I'm to blame." She pounded out some dough, probably pretending it was my face.

I had gone to bed without supper many nights because of my antics. I often wondered why my mother disliked me so much and could only conclude she blamed me for my father's disappearance years ago.

I was only five when I last saw Pa. He had to go away on business, and Ma was furious that she had to stay home from Mrs. Anne Rochester's annual masquerade ball to look after me.

"Mrs. Whittle will be there, surely looking to step in as head chairwoman, of which I am in the running for. I simply must be there, William. Just hire someone to watch her."

"Lorraine, I have missed too many business meetings

as it is. If you'd like to continue with these parties that cost me a fortune to fund, then stay home with the girl for a few days," Father had said, and left.

He never returned.

Ma and I had to move to the little town of Moss Grove after that because we couldn't afford the lush life of the city. Pa's money had disappeared with him, and my mother didn't take well to the change of living in a three-room cabin with dirt floors, baking her own bread, and not attending lavish parties, other than a church picnic. She resented me. If it weren't for me, she could have run away and remarried, once again living a prosperous life.

The setting sun painted the sky in remarkable hues of purple and orange as I made my way past the shops, pushing the memory of my father to the back of my mind. I needed to focus on the task at hand. People were mounting their horses and carriages to head home for the night. If they saw me leave town, it would get back to Ma, so I ducked through an alley between Tom's General Store and the Moss Grove Inn. No one saw as I changed into pants and climbed the fence. My feet thumped against the grass, and I ran until there was no light except the moon.

It was April eighth, 1895, my seventeenth birthday. Ma, of course, made no mention of it. She never did. It was a wonder I knew my age at all. Year after year I'd wake up, remember, and cry, knowing no one would hug me and wish me a happy birthday. I'd dress myself and go about my day, wallowing in self-pity. But the night I went to Gelid Lake for the first time was different. That morning I made a pact with myself to finally accept my mother's disdain for me. I didn't want to spend the rest of my life lonely and miserable.

I skipped along the grassy woodland floor and inhaled the smell of the pine trees lining the path, pretending they were cheering me on my special day. I had a silly thought as I moved along: what if people wrote poems and stories about me? Nathalia of the Trees is what I'd want to be called. The girl who climbed the world's most perilous trees and lived to tell the tale, or the girl who climbed so high she touched a cloud.

"Oh my gosh," I gasped as the mother of all trees came into view. It wasn't only that which drew my eye but the lake, as still as a lioness, ready to pounce upon her prey. My skin prickled with uncertainty. My heart beat harder the longer I stared, as if begging me to return to the warmth of my bed.

I set my pack on the ground and took a sip from the canteen. The water was warm and tasted of leather, but I gulped it down anyway. I shook away all doubt, eyed the first branch, and marched to it.

It was easy. So were the second, third, and fourth. The fifth was more difficult, but I made it up with only a scrape on my elbow from the bark. Hoisting my way higher and higher, I saw the full moon between the leaves. My goal was to reach a point where I could see all of it and most of the sky.

"Is that the best you got?" I yelled to the tree. *I should probably get friends, but that's on my to-do list.*

The tree fought back. I put too much confidence into my climbing abilities, and my foot slipped on a skinnier branch. I clawed at the upper branch, managing to grip it tightly, and tried to steady my palpitating heart. I had fallen from trees before, but not from this high up.

"I'm sorry," I grunted and pulled myself to the safety of a thicker branch. Why would I apologize to a tree? I sat for a moment and closed my eyes, inhaling the fresh air to calm my nerves. I pulled the moon chart from my pocket and decided, from the position of the moon in the sky, that I must've been climbing for at least an hour. A feeling of triumph washed over me. I looked to the ground, but it was blocked by limbs and leaves. I was incredibly high up, but I wasn't done. I pocketed the paper and decided to be more careful.

I may be here until sunrise, but this is worth Ma's rant about how a young lady should behave.

I wasn't much good at anything else. I burnt any food Ma made me cook, understanding most of my school assignments was difficult, I couldn't make a hit in our schoolyard baseball games, and I was too nervous to talk to people. I think that made Ma the maddest.

"How are you to get a well-bred husband if you can't even do something as simple as make a friend?" She, of course, wanted a rich husband for me so she didn't have to wear "rags," as she called them. I thought the dresses were simple and lovely, but that was yet another difference between us.

As my boots scuffed along the branches, I remembered the first tree I climbed. Eight years ago, Matilda Mae was skipping rope behind the school. Her curls hopped down her back as she jumped, and her smile was radiant. I wanted to experience her happiness, so I asked if I could play. A boy named Charlie Dewin cackled from behind me.

"Matilda wouldn't be seen with the likes of a simpleton," he scoffed.

My eyes burned with tears. I knew I wasn't good at socializing, but how could someone be so mean?

"Stop it, Charlie," Matilda chided, but it was too late. I would have rather slept in a cabbage patch than let those kids see me cry. I ran until a tree with low-hanging branches stood in front of me. I jumped up and climbed until the leaves hid me. It was there that I cried, alone and hidden. From then on, I wanted to climb every tree I could, and I felt better about myself each time.

That sycamore became my greatest expedition. Up, up I went until my breath caught in my chest. The moon's enchanting glow seemed to shine a spotlight on me. I'd done it. I made it to the top of the tallest tree. I gazed down at the lake over a hundred feet below the branch where I sat. A fresh breeze lifted my hair as if bowing to Nathalia of the Trees. I'd closed my eyes and smiled when a noise startled me – a yelp of some sort.

A silver fox gazed up and growled. Even though it would take me another hour to climb down, I wouldn't dare try if it was still there. He stood on the other side of the small lake – more like the size of a pond – screaming at me. Then he did something I never thought was possible: he jumped right into the lake and swam to the base of the tree. He shook off and continued barking without a sign of frostbite.

Another breeze, colder this time, swirled around me like it was alive and angry. I screamed and clung to the trunk while the wind shoved me.

"Stop!" I begged, but it only grew stronger. The branch beneath me cracked loudly, and I fell from the tree, smacking branches all the way down. I grappled, trying to catch hold of just one branch, but my hands kept slipping. Suddenly, my back hit the water with incredible force, knocking the air from my lungs. Cold enveloped my body which convulsed and fought for air. I kicked and waved my arms, trying to reach the surface, my lungs burning. Before I could reach the top, I sucked in a gulp of water and darkness took me.

I don't know how long I was in the water before I awoke, floating below the blue surface. A small glow floated from far off below the lake toward me, then it broke off into many glowing orbs. The closer they came, I saw that they were some sort of human-like creatures with wings like fins and webbed fingers and toes. My body wasn't breathing, but it seemed it didn't need to. The beings swam around my head and took turns kissing my cheeks with tiny, cold lips, spreading warmth throughout my body, and I fell unconscious.

When I came to, I was outside the fence of Moss Grove, bone dry with my canteen at my side and my dress skirts still shoved behind a bush where I left them. Was it possible it had been a dream? Perhaps I had fallen from the fence as I was leaving town, and I hadn't climbed the sycamore. No, it was real. I felt it in my heart.

I snuck into my house and crawled into bed. Maybe I could make sense of this after a good night's sleep.

It felt more like a dream than ever when I awoke from a restless night. I was desperate to investigate the lake, this time during the day.

Chapter Two
The Silver Fox

"You're lucky no one saw, stupid girl." Ma slopped chunky-looking oatmeal into a bowl the next morning. "I have never, in my life, had a poor reputation. William and I should have given you up when we had the chance."

I should have cried at her ferocious words, but I was used to them. Father had never taken much of a liking to me, either, according to her. Since I didn't have many memories of him, I could at least imagine he liked me for the five years he was in my life. I wanted to say something snarky, like "Fine, give me away, then. It'd be better than living here." But I knew she'd only get angrier.

A knock sounded at the door, and Ma changed her attitude real quick. She smoothed her hair, plastered on a smile, and opened it to a man with a fancy suit and top hat.

"Morning, ma'am."

"Mr. Jonas, come in."

I looked from him to her. Ma never had gentlemen callers.

"Mr. Jonas is your new tutor. He'll make sure you … succeed."

I knew she meant he was more of a babysitter.

"I'm no longer in school, Ma. And anyway, how can you afford this?" The question slipped out, and the fury in Ma's eyes told me to shut up.

"Quite an inappropriate question in front of a perfect stranger, girl," Mr. Jonas said. He turned to Ma. "I see I have my work cut out for me."

This was going to be my own personal Hell.

Mr. Jonas tutored me for weeks in the most important subjects: how to sit straight in a chair and not move while spooning soup into my mouth – something I failed at multiple times. He tapped my hand with his cane every time I slurped. I learned how to walk with my head held high, and curtsy. I was informed it wasn't proper to speak until spoken to, which was a hard one for me since I always ask too many questions.

"Etiquette, Nathalia, is what will get you to the top."

"Of a tree?" I snickered until he slapped the table and pushed up from his chair.

"Ms. Richards, there is a finishing school for young ladies in the northern part of the city. If there is any hope for this girl, that is where she must go."

Ma looked at me. "How long would she be there?"

"Long enough."

Long enough for what?

"You may go, Nathalia. Mr. Jonas and I have a lot to discuss."

I ran from the cabin, wanting to get back to the lake to inspect it. Mr. Jonas had kept such a close eye on me I couldn't even sneak out at night. He took a room at the inn and caught me heading for the gate a few times and sent me straight back home.

Since he was occupied with my mother, planning the most horrendous future for me at the moment, I had nothing to stop me.

That is, until I reached the gate and my stomach curled. A headache blinded me, and I heard distant voices as I collapsed on the ground. I awoke in bed to hear Ma arguing with someone.

"It's just a little cold. It will pass."

"Ms. Richards, I really insist I fetch the doctor."

"No."

Two days passed, and I was falling more ill, but Ma still refused the doctor. If I died, she'd be free of me.

The pain in my head drowned out most of the noise from the outside world. But as I laid there, probably dying, an odd sensation overwhelmed me, and I had the sudden urge to flee the cabin and take refuge in the woods. As I tried to convince myself to be rational, a scream-like howl came from outside my window. I mustered the energy to slip from the bed and hobble to the window.

My vision blurred, but I couldn't mistake the silver fox staring up at me. It wasn't the fever-causing hallucinations. He was there, and he wanted something. I covered my nightgown with a robe and pulled on my boots.

Ma wasn't in the house, so slipping out was easy. I hugged myself for warmth as my eyes locked on the fox's. He turned, looked back at me for a second, then trotted toward the trail leading away from Moss Grove. I followed.

It seemed as if my fever was letting up slightly, and I couldn't help but think it was because of this creature. What an odd thought. I walked behind him on a small trail I hadn't seen before, one that circled the outskirts of town. I peeked over the fence when I heard Ma's voice. She and Mr. Jonas were arm in arm, walking out of the inn's restaurant. The fox's bark forced me to look away and continue on.

The hour and a half walk was brutal on my tired body. I knew he was taking me back to the tree, and I couldn't resist the compulsion to follow. I put my fist to my mouth and coughed. My knees gave out and I fell, tumbling forward into the dirt, chilled from the night air. The fox barreled toward my body and circled it once. The breeze he made was strong and flowed through me, its strange warmth coaxing me to continue on. When we finally arrived, I sagged at the base of the great sycamore. My head rested against the tree as I caught my breath. Then I looked at the fox.

"What is it you want?" I breathed.

The fox stared at me, his eyes weren't of any animal I'd ever seen. That peculiar wind came again and swirled around the animal, engulfing him in a silver-tinted fog. I gasped and froze in place, the spiky grass poking through my nightdress. From the fog stepped a boy around my age with silvery-blond hair. I was right about his eyes – they were human.

I couldn't run. I couldn't even move.

"You act like you've never seen a guardian before." His voice was deep, smooth, and had a hint of sarcasm.

"A what?" My body shook with fear at those intense, bright eyes bearing down on me.

He raised his brows before he looked me up and down, as if what he saw was pathetic. I was pathetic, sitting there whimpering uncontrollably.

"*This* is what the sprites send me? You're shuddering like a thistle about to be eaten by a rabbit." The boy turned to the lake. "I'd be better off partnering with an armadillo," he shouted at the unmoving water. He faced me once more and put his hands on his hips. "I'll have to deal with it. Alright, kid, go take a drink." He pointed back to the lake.

I looked from him to the water, then back to him, appalled. "Are you serious?"

"You're sick."

"Clearly." I coughed a ball of phlegm into my fist, conveniently timed.

"You must drink from the lake, or you'll never recover." He squared his shoulders coolly, like this somehow wasn't the most absurd, inconceivable thing a person could say. My mother telling me she loves me would have shocked me less.

"You're joshing me."

"You wanna die? Fine. I'm better off on my own, as I always have been. They should see this was a mistake by now."

They? "The shimmering webbed creatures in the water?" I asked.

"No, the slug sitting beside you." He nodded to my side where a slug, indeed, rested on a leaf.

"Ick!" I inched away as fast as my frail body would allow.

"Wow." The boy was unenthusiastic, to say the least. He rolled his eyes to the sky, then lowered his chin until he was nearly glaring at me.

"I need to go home," I said, feeling faint. He huffed and stomped to the edge of the lake, scooped up water in his hands, and brought it to me. I scrunched my face at the thought of drinking dirty lake water out of a stranger's hands.

"Drink or die, girl." The boy's voice had an urgency that made me comply.

I brought my lips to the side of his hand and let the water slip into my mouth. It was more refreshing than the springs in Moss Grove. It had a faint sweetness, a taste I couldn't put a word to besides *nature* – all the good scents and tastes of Earth. The cool water flowed down my throat, chest, and into my stomach, and with its smooth movement, I felt strength. It was healing water. Once his hands were empty, I looked up at the boy.

"Better?" he asked, wiping his hands on the leather tunic he wore overtop a white shirt, quite an odd outfit.

"Tell me what's going on." I sat up on my knees, ready to pound him with every question bombarding my mind.

"You've been chosen, for some unknown, ridiculous reason." He glared back at Gelid Lake like it was a living being.

"Chosen for what? And who are you?"

"Cole."

"Cole *what*?" Now that I was feeling better, I was more annoyed than anything, and I was almost grateful because it outshined the fear.

"Just Cole. And you are?"

"Nathalia."

"Prettier name than a weed, I'll admit." The moon

16

brightened his silver hair as I blushed unwillingly at the compliment.

"Will you tell me now – why I'm here? And how in the world you ... you—"

"Transformed from a fox?" He sat on the ground a few feet from me and rested his arms on his raised knees. "I'm a Guardian of the Curse, an immortal."

My eyes widened and I waited.

He snorted a laugh. "I've never explained this in my whole existence. I shouldn't have to now." He leaned his head toward the water again and said in a heightened voice, "I'm perfectly capable on my own!" Cole paused, like he was waiting for an answer, then directed his attention back to me. "The Shkraykh are hungry. There aren't enough guilty prisoners for them to feast on, so they've become even more feral than they already are. I guess the sprites think I'm not strong enough to keep the creatures in the gorge by myself." He huffed like a child not getting his way.

"Slow down. Shkraykh? Prisoners? *Feast!*" I gulped.

"You'll be battling the creatures beside me now. Not sure how a wimpy little thistle will do in the presence of the Shkraykh."

I curled my lip and wrinkled my nose, resisting the urge to stomp home. Being in his company was unpleasant, but my curiosity consumed me. I was certainly not planning on battling anything or anyone.

"You look fine, now." Cole stood, wiping bits of

leaves off of his black pants. "Go home. I'll be back for you in a month." He walked past the tree.

"Wait," I said, pushing myself off the ground and smacking my hands together to clean the dirt off. "Why a month?"

He grumbled and marched back. "You have to drink the lake water each month on the full moon until it's Feast Day. Or you'll die." He shrugged.

It was a lot to take in, and I wasn't sure I believed him. I was sick, delirious. I must have imagined a fox and stumbled into the woods to find a crazy man roaming around. I crossed my arms, entertaining the silver-haired weirdo for a moment longer. "And when is this feast day?"

"A little less than a year. See ya." He walked behind a tree, silver fog trailing behind him, leaving me baffled, unsure, and miffed. I trudged home, kicking mushrooms and pretending they were Cole's stupid head.

So rude, I thought, slapping a mosquito between my hands. "Well now he's gone, and I can get on with my life," I concluded as I entered my town's gates. Ma hadn't noticed I was gone. She was humming a song in her bedroom when I sneaked in.

It was just before dusk when I awoke the next day. Ma was at the table, busy scribbling letters.

"Sleeping all day is lazy and will *not* be tolerated at the finishing school," she said without looking at me.

"I'm sorry."

She glanced up this time and narrowed her eyes like I was up to some mischief.

"Do you need help?" I nodded to whatever she was writing. "I can run them to the post office."

"No." She went back to the letters.

"Can I take my journal out to the fields? I'm still feeling woozy, but the fresh air will help."

"It's almost dark."

"I won't climb trees, and I won't sit on the grass. I'll stay on the bench and sit like a lady." I'd say anything to get out of there.

"Fine, Nathalia," she snapped.

I didn't lie about the trees. I had no desire to climb. I only wanted to be alone with my thoughts. My memory was hazy, but that boy, Cole – his nearly glowing eyes and silver hair flitted through my mind.

"Nutcase," I mumbled, hopping over a log near a small swamp within our town, not wanting to go to the field at all. The frogs croaked, the flies buzzed, and the little fish splashed.

Cole's deep voice sounded in my head as I remembered his strange words, "You've been chosen, for some unknown and ridiculous reason."

I didn't choose to entertain the thought of what he said, rather it invaded my mind, until my attention was drawn to the skinny trees sparsely placed about the area. Rustling, like a deer, came from somewhere amongst the brambles.

No deer venture through here, I thought, knowing there was no food for them. I inched closer, keeping quiet like I usually did when I hid from Ma or my peers in the woods.

"Cole?" I said aloud when I saw a silver, bushy tail. The minute the name slipped from my lips, I shook my head, knowing it had to be impossible.

Transform.

I stopped walking, wondering if the voice I'd just heard was real.

Transform, Nathalia. The words were in my mind. But the way he said my name ... it was Cole.

"I don't know how," I dared to reply.

You do. Just close your eyes and let your true self take over.

My true self? This *had* to be impossible. The crystal-eyed boy was a stranger in the woods, not a mystical fox. And yet, I thought about my true self ... I inhaled deeply and exhaled slowly and closed my eyes, imagining myself as a fox. I felt foolish at first, but the image of a slim, silver fox with *my* eyes became so vivid in my head, it was like I was seeing it for real.

Good, the voice said.

Are you the boy from last night? I silently asked, wondering if I was communicating or just talking to myself.

I have a name, girl. It was definitely Cole with that snarky reply.

As do I. I kept my eyes closed, watching my fox form pounce around in my mind.

Okay, little thistle. The sprites told me to take you hunting. So, let's get on with it.

My eyes shot open at the absurd words. I turned to make my way home, wanting to go back to sleep to clear my head, when I realized I was shorter. I made eye contact with a squirrel at the base of a tree. I tried to stand, thinking I'd fallen to the ground, but no … I *was* standing – on all four legs, in fact. I screamed, my audible voice animalistic, my inner voice packed with human panic.

Relax, girl.

I yelped, bounced, fell, and rolled.

I said RELAX. The silver fox appeared in front of me, snarling.

I laid on the ground, breathing in and out, trying to do as he said.

Find your voice.

I yelped again.

Inner voice, he growled.

It took me more than a minute. *Help,* I said.

I'm trying, but you're impossible!

What did you do to me? I asked.

I did nothing, and if I could reverse this and send you home to live out your mundane human life, I would.

A wave of anger swept over me at his words, at his tone. *So, I was chosen,* I said, standing to face him. *And there's nothing you can do about it?*

Unfortunately, not.

I barked at his insulting tone, suddenly embracing the overwhelming, thrilling feeling of a challenge. *Let's hunt, then.* I followed Cole beyond the swamp to a thicker forest, then into a field outside of town.

There, to the right, he said.

Rabbits?

Do you know anything about foxes? He moved forward. *I'll try not to let them munch on you, thistle.*

I growled but followed.

Stay low, he commanded, readying himself to pounce, though I knew a rabbit couldn't outrun a fox.

The thought of killing and eating an animal without cooking it should have sickened me, but my animal self-craved meat. I was right, it wasn't tough to catch them. My human self *would* be sick after eating the raw meat, fur and all, but with these new taste buds?

Was it good?

Yes. I swirled happily.

Cole then grew taller and less furry. He spoke out loud, but I didn't understand him. It was like another language.

Human form, he said in my mind.

I closed my eyes and opened them. Nothing happened. Cole huffed and tapped his foot.

It's my first time! I argued, still trying to get myself back to normal.

I'm going to wash up. Meet me at the creek when you finally figure it out. He walked in the opposite direction, but I heard him mumble, *Useless. Absolutely useless.* The fact that he didn't speak it out loud told me he wanted me to hear his words.

Jerk. I knew he heard me when he shot me a glaring look, then continued walking.

I squeezed my eyes shut and felt the wind on my face becoming colder, and I realized I'd lost my fur. I was human again, but with the new sight of a nocturnal animal. It wasn't as dark as it was before. Cole moved further away, but I wasn't going to follow that boy. I flared my nostrils and stuck out my tongue, even though he didn't see, and started back toward Moss Grove.

"Oh no you don't!" He grabbed my arm and swung me around. His face was so close that I blinked, unsure of what to do.

"How'd you move so fast?" I asked, looking over his shoulder where I had just seen him at least sixty feet away.

"A rabbit is the opposite of a threat, not even close to what you'll be dealing with. We have more training." He let go, ignoring my question, and I stumbled back.

"And if I choose not to?"

"I already told you what would happen." Cole continued to the creek, somehow knowing I'd follow. I was too curious for my own good. He positioned himself on a small lump of grass and pointed at the clear,

23

running water. "Catch one."

I blew out air, not ready to go through another crazy transformation.

"As a human," he said, likely reading my facial expression.

"That's impossible." *So is everything that's happened thus far.*

He shrugged and chewed on a long blade of grass. I rolled up my sleeves, shooting him another look of irritation, and stepped into the water, waiting for a trout to appear.

Chapter Three
The Shkraykh

"Enough." Cole threw down the fifth blade of grass he'd gnawed on and stood. "Over an hour and you can't even touch a fish."

"I'm not a bear!"

"No, but you *do* have the instincts of a fox. Tap into them."

I scoffed, crossing my arms over my chest.

"Watch," he whispered, positioning himself next to me. The light breeze carried his scent to my nostrils – sandalwood. I swallowed, briefly shifting my gaze to his eyes, shimmering with the reflection of the water we stood in, then focused on the stream trickling over small rocks beneath us. It took two seconds for him to clap into the water, snatching up a large, flailing, green trout, but his grip was strong. "See?" Cole released the fish and motioned for me to try again.

I hunched down, my hands open and ready.

"No, no. Like this." The boy touched my back and held my arm, moving me into a crouch. The entire bottom of my skirts were soaked, but I ignored it for now. He put a finger to his lips, and I closed my eyes, listening to the calm waters, and pictured myself as a fox snapping up a fish.

"Finally, you did something right."

I hadn't noticed the fish clutched in my wet hands until I opened my eyes. "I did it!" I let go of the fish and splashed around in a circle, whooping at my success. When I'd composed myself, Cole stood cross-armed, watching me.

"You done?" he asked, raising one brow.

"You don't look very proud of me," I teased, more to bother him than anything.

"Sublimely proud." Sarcasm seemed to be his only response. I squeezed my skirts, wringing out the water, and sat on a rock, untying my soggy boots.

"*If* I agree to battling these Shkooras or whatever they're called, you have to tell me about them." I wiggled my bare toes in the grass.

"They're called *Sh-crake*," he said, emphasizing the pronunciation. Cole leaned against a tree with a hand in his pocket. "They were once women, cursed while standing on the sacred ground of Vastaya."

I wrinkled my nose.

"They were a coven of witches, ones who practiced things ... *other* than healing."

I shivered, the thought of witches terrifying me.

"What the Shkraykh coven didn't know was that the

26

ground in which they performed their ritual sacrifice wasn't to be touched, let alone disturbed with the corpses of their victims."

"Disturbed with the corpses of their victims," I said in distaste at the word.

"The field belonged to the sprites —"

"The sprites?"

He tilted his head, annoyed at my interruption. "The sprites enchanted the land to forever provide creatures of Earth with food, warmth, and safety."

"Enchanted land," I repeated with awe, wanting to see what it looked like.

"Do you have any original thoughts or have you become my echo?"

"Sorry, go on." I settled in and shut my mouth.

"Directly after the ritual was complete, before the coven could leave the field, the ground shook. It was an earthquake confined to the sacred ground only. It caved in, dropping the Shkraykh deep into a newly crafted gorge."

"Did they die?"

"Nathalia," Cole warned, and I swiped my fingers over my lips in a zipping motion. He lowered himself to the grass beside the rock. "They didn't die, but their lives were taken. The sprites mourned their land and watched as the women clad in black gowns turned pale. Their skin turned to wrinkled leather – their eyes hollowed. They screeched like banshees, wallowing in their forever

27

misery. They were no longer human, but creatures of the curse."

"How long have you been the ... uh,"

"Guardian of the Curse?" He shrugged. "Two hundred years or so. Can't remember."

"How old are you?"

"Eighteen. Or two hundred. Either works."

My eyes widened with shock, as if I thought the information couldn't get more nonsensical.

The medieval outfit makes sense, now, I thought, running my eyes from the collar of his shirt and down the leather tunic.

His sudden motion grabbed my attention as he shot his gaze to the moon, bright and high in the sky.

"Go home," he said, standing from the ground and pulling me to my feet.

"What about the story?" I asked, studying his eyes, glazed with worry.

"Another time. Go."

"Cole, what is it?"

"It's late," he said, pointing to the sky.

"So?"

"So, you have human parents who will ask questions if you've disappeared for hours into the night. You must make sure no one knows – that no one asks. Got it? Go home," he said again, "and I'll tell you the rest next time."

"When is next time?" I questioned, not mentioning I

only had an absent mother, but the silver wind had captured him, and the fox fled to the woods.

Days passed, and the nights dragged on, and I began to believe it truly was my imagination. It was easy to think – becoming a fox? Dead witch creatures? *Just me dreaming up adventures, once again*, I thought, knowing it was a habit of mine when the loneliness became too overwhelming. Creating handsome boys who'd whisk me away to do something exciting. That was me.

"Did you hear me, Nathalia?"

"What?"

Ma stared at me with her flour-covered hands on her hips.

"I'm sorry, Ma," I said, focusing on kneading the wad of dough in front of me.

She lit a fire in our stone fireplace. "I said we've set a date for your departure."

"Right. Finishing school." I'd finished with the dough and handed it to Ma for the pan.

"You leave within the month."

"Within the ... so soon?" I exclaimed.

"You're seventeen and already far behind the other girls your age. The sooner you go, the better."

Better for you, I thought with a bit of an ache in my heart. "Can I go outside now?"

Ma nodded but didn't look at me. I untied my apron and hung it on a hook, laced my boots, and closed the door behind me, inhaling the late spring air. If what happened to me *was* true, I could only blame my need to be outside on the animal inside me. A fox needs to run free, not be locked up baking bread and learning the various types of stitches. And especially not at finishing school, learning how to be a proper lady.

I heard my name called as I was making my way to the town gates.

"Nathalia?" Charlie Dewin approached me with his hands in his pockets. He toed the dirt, looking shy. "I wanted to apologize for the way I've treated you in the past."

I blinked at the suddenness of his words. If he wasn't teasing me daily, he ignored me. Just yesterday, he'd bumped my shoulder when walking by and continued on as if I'd been invisible.

He held out his rough-looking hand, offering me his arm. "Walk with me?"

"I'm busy." I made to move past him.

"I know I was mean to you," he said, stopping me in my tracks.

"Why were you?" I asked.

"This is no excuse, but I liked you, Nathalia."

"*Me*?"

He nodded. "You're intriguing, and beautiful." He pushed my hair behind my ear, making me shiver. I was useless in close-contact situations, it seemed, and I couldn't determine if I was uncomfortable, or just shocked. Should I run? Should I hear him out?

What would Ma say if she knew some boy liked me and wanted to walk with me? Probably that I should accept and marry the first man with money who would have me.

He took my hand, placing it on his arm, making the decision for me, and led me toward the swamp, *my* swamp – the one place no one in town ever visited. It was smelly, but it was my place of refuge when the treetops wouldn't do. I fidgeted with a lock of hair, wildly nervous as he continued to compliment me and apologize.

"Do you forgive me?" He gazed at me.

All I could do was give a weak smile, and we continued on as he doted on me with endless flattery.

"If I could climb a tree like you, phew, I'd be the top hunter. Rodrick would be jealous of that. Will you teach me?"

"Um …"

"Here we are," he said without waiting for my answer. The muddy pond sat just beyond our feet.

"You wouldn't believe the *frogs* we catch here." He said 'frogs' oddly, and soon I found out why. It was a signal. A group of boys emerged from behind trees and bushes, malicious grins on their ugly faces.

I gulped and tried to back away, but Charlie stood

behind me. I turned, hoping he hadn't lied, and that he'd protect me. Instead, he held an old, wrinkled paper with a sketch of a girl in a tree ... my sketch.

"Nathalia of the Trees," he laughed, clutching his stomach like it was the funniest thing he'd seen. "What are you, a squirrel?"

"No, she's a racoon. They live amongst trash," one boy said, crunching the leaves as he moved forward.

"Nah, racoons are nice and fat. She's just a skinny, ugly, little bug with a brain to match." With that, Charlie pushed me into the mud. His friends trudged through, kicking the thick goop all over me as I cried out and covered my face with my hands.

"Charlie, let's get out of here!" As quickly as they emerged into the clearing, the boys disappeared. A howl hit my caked-up ears. I wiped the mud from my eyes to see Cole step into the swamp.

He pulled me up by the elbow. "What did I tell you about keeping a low profile?" he scolded while I swiped the caked mud from my blue dress.

"I'm not allowed to be around people at all, now?" I spit muck from my mouth.

He drew his head back, his entire face contorted like he was befuddled. "Those are the types of people you keep as company?" He shook his head and stepped out of the pond. "I suppose you were just playing a game, then." Cole motioned at me.

Angry tears welled in my eyes. I wanted to go home

where no one could see me break down as the dialogue ran through my mind.

Skinny.

Ugly.

Racoon.

Bug.

Trash.

"Follow me." Cole's voice pierced through my tormentors' ghostly insults. I inhaled and wiped my eyes while his back was turned. He glanced over his shoulder, and for a split second, I saw pity on his face. I considered leaving, but the proof I'd been searching for was walking toward Gelid Lake, so I trailed behind, fighting the tears.

"If you transform, it'll be easier to get clean," he said once we arrived at the stationary, blue water.

"I'll get frostbite." I knelt by the water's edge.

"You don't remember drinking it, apparently. Wouldn't expect much more from a thistle."

"Shut up!" I screamed, to his surprise. He held up his palms in surrender, backing away as if I'd bite him. I wanted to, but I instead thought about my animal – my silky, silver fur, the heightened senses allowing me to smell the grass deeper, and to see the intricate details on a butterfly's wings. Seeing my paws in front of me, I stepped forward and swam through the warm water of the otherwise frozen Gelid Lake. If animals could weep, I'd shrivel up from dehydration. I lapped up the sweet water, wanting to feel strength rather than my constant weakness. Cole sat by the sycamore, waiting. I climbed out and shook my fur, then transformed into my old, skinny, bug-brained self. My damp hair hung around my face like a curtain as I stared at the grains of dirt between the green grass blades. The air was still and quiet except for a chickadee singing in the distance.

"Are we done feeling sorry for ourselves?" Cole approached me, waiting for my reply.

"Go away," I whispered.

He puffed out air. "Gladly." Before he could take even a step away, chimes sounded and the water rippled like pebbles had been skipped across the surface.

"*Fine*," he said to the lake, then faced me. "The sprites need me to take you to the gorge. So, get those idiots out of your mind, clear it, because what you're going to see will shock you to your core."

Chapter Four
The Gorge

Cole stopped at the edge of a cliff, but I couldn't move. My eyes were glued to the sight before me. A long beam, secured to the edge of two cliffs, ran the length of a crater, which was a few hundred yards wide, at least. Hundreds of nooses hung like party streamers across the beam. Some were empty, some were splattered with age-old blood. Some still had decomposing corpses, and some only had bits of skeletal remains.

The wind blew, carrying with it the stench of rotting flesh. I gagged, ready to retch all over the dirt that dusted my boots.

"Hold it in, Nathalia," Cole said. "It'll be worse when fresh men hang here, waiting to become a meal for the Shkraykh." He pointed to a raised bed of black dirt at the bottom of the two cliff walls. "That's where they emerge on Feast Day."

"They live beneath the ground?"

"They lay dormant, hibernating until the Feast Day moon wakes them."

"And what is it you do?" I asked, pulling my eyes from the atrocious scene.

"My job is to make sure they never leave this gorge. If they do, the surrounding towns are doomed. They wouldn't get much further since the rising sun calls them back to their graves."

I forced myself to glance at the beam again. "Where did they come from?" I motioned at the human remains.

Cole squinted into the sun, its rays brightening his eyes, making them look almost white. "In the city next to us, Harburgh, the Feast Day is confidential knowledge. Only a group of officials, the Luminary, know about it." His eyes moved to mine. "For the past couple hundred years, they've sacrificed prisoners to the Shkraykh."

"That's awful," I yelped, imagining their not so swift deaths. I pictured a man dangling from the noose, struggling to escape, while a witch tore into his flesh.

"You're a bad guy sympathizer, huh? Those men deserved far worse than being a main course."

"Do you have to be so graphic," I spewed, trying to force the visuals from my mind.

"This is exactly what I was talking about. You don't have the stomach for this, nor the bravery."

"I didn't ask for any of this!" I yelled back, waving my hands at our surroundings.

He marched over until he towered above me, glaring at me with wild eyes. "You can't even handle stupid, untrue insults from insignificant humans. The sprites thought you were special enough to be chosen, yet you take the words of those imbeciles as truth instead of realizing you were destined for greatness. Find your voice, Nathalia, or you'll never succeed as a guardian."

He stalked off toward the lake, his boots scuffing through the dirt in a manner that told me he was more frustrated than angry. He probably thought I wasn't taking any of this seriously – putting my human emotions before everything else. I suppose he thought I'd immediately accept my fate – that I was no longer entirely human. *Could* I accept it as my truth? Could I admit it was all real, and not a vivid form of my imagination?

Yes, my inner voice said, and I embraced it instinctively. I came to the realization that, though the dangers and fears were imminent, and though I'd only been a fox a couple of times, it was somehow fulfilling. I wouldn't admit it out loud, but I looked forward to spending time with Cole. He was a grouch, but an entertaining one. I almost liked how easily I could get under his skin.

I looked at him for a moment before running to catch up.

You were destined for greatness. His words soaked into my mind, and I smiled.

"Was that a compliment?" I asked.

"How did you come to that conclusion?" he snapped.

"You said the nasty things they said about me aren't

true and told me I was special." I chuckled, my mind feeling weightless. It felt like I finally had a friend.

"You twisted my words." He kept his attention on where he was going, stomping the ground harder.

"Find your voice," I repeated his words. "I'll take your challenge." I skipped beside him until he paused, his face contorted with annoyance.

"I didn't challenge you to anything." His nostrils flared, making it all the more thrilling.

"You think I'm equal to a flimsy weed – a thistle whose only purpose is to become food for a rabbit."

He raised a brow.

"I'm going to show you I'm a rose – the tallest one with the thickest stem. I'll have the sharpest thorns, and – " I stood on tiptoe to level my eyes with his. "I'll be the sweetest smelling of them all." I flipped my hair and spun around, leaving him standing in silence – dumbfounded, almost as I was, at my newfound audacious manner.

The minute I closed my front door, I burst into laughter. It was the best I'd ever felt – powerful … and maybe even older. I was already a young adult at the age of seventeen, but I finally felt like it. I no longer felt like a little girl, clawing her way through life to find her purpose.

"What's gotten into you?" Ma asked, turning the corner and giving me a quizzical look.

"I feel good, better than ever, in fact." I controlled my giggling, but I couldn't wipe away my smile as the image of Cole and his stupefied face hung in my mind. Rabbits and fish? I couldn't wait for the next assignment.

"You look pale." Ma said it like an insult. "Mr. Jonas will be joining us for dinner. Be on your best behavior, young lady. Show him you're worthy of going to such a fine school."

I'd made it home for dinner. *Good. Cole said to keep a low profile, I can do that.*

Mr. Jonas sipped his tea as he told us about the school and what to expect, and it sounded awful. "Will you pass the biscuits, Nathalia?"

As our knuckles touched, Mr. Jonas dropped the entire basket and covered his hand against his chest, staring at me. "Your hand is cold as ice," he gasped.

I glanced at it. My skin was paler than normal, but I didn't feel cold.

"We must fetch the doctor," he demanded. When Ma questioned why, he said, "If the school detects any illness, they will not take her. Would you like to be strapped with this heathen forever?"

To my dismay, my mother told him to get Doc Wilson.

"Stay," she said as I climbed into bed. I felt just fine.

"How are you, young lady?" Doc Wilson asked as he entered my room. He set his leather bag on the floor and pulled out the stethoscope. He shook his head after silently listening to my heartbeat and moved it to the left, then the right, then down.

"That's odd." He took the stethoscope out of his ears and turned hesitantly to my ma. "I can't seem to hear a heartbeat."

Ma drew her head back and looked at me, commenting on how I've paled even more in the last few hours. Doc Wilson tried again, but alas, no beating heart. He tested the stethoscope on himself, then tried it on me again.

I put my hand to my chest. "I can feel it, I'm fine."

He gripped my wrist with two fingers and scrunched his brow. "Mrs. Richards,"

"*Miss,*" she corrected.

"I have no words." He stood, fear etched across his face, his lips thin. "I must consult my textbooks and speak with my colleagues."

"What's wrong with her?" Ma asked, panic in her voice. I could almost imagine her worry was for my life.

Almost.

"Ms. Richards," he said, shaking his head slightly like he didn't know what to say. "I'm not sure how it's possible, but your daughter has no pulse."

Chapter Five
Forever Young

I ran from the house, barefoot and frightened. Ma chased me, calling for me to get back or she'd get the switch. I dashed through the town faster than I'd ever gone, and though I moved at incredible speed, I could clearly hear the words the people spoke as I passed through.

"Was that the Richards girl?"

"The odd one, I think it was."

"She was barefoot!"

"Indecent."

"Wild."

I didn't care what they said. *Insignificant*, I told myself as I focused on reaching Gelid Lake. I ran so fast I couldn't stop before splashing into the water, up to my knees.

"Cole?" I called out. Again and again, I screamed his name until he finally appeared.

"What is wrong with you?" He swept that ash-blond hair from his face as he stepped into the clearing.

"I'm dead. I'm dead." I couldn't hide my frenzy.

"Is that all?"

"Is that … this is sort of a big deal to me, Cole! How am I dead but alive?"

"You're becoming immortal. Your living body is being replaced with stronger blood and a tenacious heart, one that will never stop beating."

Never stop beating, immortal. "Alive until the end of all time," I whispered, then stepped out of the water. I could only stare at the ground as reality set in. I would never grow old. I'd never get sick, and I'd never, ever die.

"You're not acting very *rosy* right now."

"Shut up," I demanded, then shook it off. "What happens when everyone notices I'm not aging? Doc Wilson is already going to consult with other doctors about my lack of a pulse, and –"

"What did you say?"

"I said I don't have a pulse."

"Doc Wilson came to you?"

I took a step back as he moved even closer, making my heart pound. "My mother noticed how cold I was, so …"

"Oh, this is bad." He spun around and paced the ground. "This is very, very bad."

The urgency in his voice frightened me. Watching him go back and forth, rubbing his chin, and the intensity in his eyes gave me chills.

"How bad?" I dared to ask.

"Doc Wilson knows."

"Like, *knows*?"

Cole nodded.

"What does it mean for us?"

"It means you failed at the one thing I told you to do! Low profile, no questions."

"Jeez, Cole, it would have been great to know I'm one of the undead! This whole situation could have been avoided."

He threw his hands into the air. "Useless!"

"Is there any other vital information you'd like to share with me so I don't get yelled at every time I see you?" I put my hands on my hips as he ground his teeth. Without warning, he grabbed my hand and yanked me after him.

"We're going to remedy this."

"How?" I wondered if his skin was cold to the touch for humans, too. I only felt its warmth. Cole glanced down and noticed me staring at his hand clutching mine, then immediately dropped it.

"You'll go home and assure your parents you're fine. I'll travel into Harburgh and spread rumors that dear old Doc Wilson has lost his marbles. Gossip travels fast, and no one will trust his word, thus saving you from prying minds and gossip."

I stopped and he turned to me. "That doesn't seem fair, to ruin a man's reputation."

"Nathalia, you're a new immortal, a baby, in a sense. You have no idea of the dangers this has put us in."

"Then explain it to me, Cole."

He rubbed his temple. "At the start of all this, the townsfolk tried to capture the sprites, wanting them to reverse the curse. The Shkraykh had mauled entire families by then. To protect themselves, the sprites made it impossible for mortals to reach them."

"By turning the lake into a freezing deathtrap."

"Precisely. Can you guess who the people wanted to trap next?"

"You?"

"Ah, you *do* have the ability to learn," he said, condescendingly.

I rolled my eyes and continued into the woods. Walking along the path lined with clover and wildflowers. My bare feet in the soft soil was peaceful, something I desperately needed at that moment.

"They thought I could break the curse, but I can't. I've successfully evaded them all these years, but stories of the Cold One continue to circulate within those with the top-secret knowledge."

"The Cold One?"

"It's what they named me. Skin cold to the touch?" He nodded at my hand.

"I've made Doc Wilson suspicious," I said, my stomach sinking.

"Yep. Well done, kid."

"You're such a grouch!" I huffed.

"I have every right to be. I've managed to keep those

witches confined in the gorge for over two centuries, then a little girl comes along and botches years' worth of work within a month."

I shoved him into a patch of poison oak. "Call me 'little girl' again and see what happens."

I'm unsure how, but at that moment, I transformed into a fox. I hadn't pictured myself as one but defending myself against that boy lit a fire within, something I never wanted to extinguish.

Cole yelled something at me in human language as I bolted through the forest, but I didn't care to find out what. I ran into the night, sniffing the sweet and earthy smells of the forest, feeling the wind fluff my fur, feeling free, though I knew I wasn't.

Chapter Six
Matilda Mae

Cole hadn't shown his face for weeks. I thought it might be because his ego was burned, but the conversation I overheard one evening between my mother and Mr. Jonas told me he'd gone into the city, after all.

"This means she's fine, correct?" Ma asked.

"Something *is* wrong with her. Have you felt her skin?"

"What do you suggest, Mr. Jonas?" I could hear her pacing the kitchen from where I sat on my bed, hoping she wouldn't look in and see me eavesdropping. She'd box my ears for sure.

"We'll send her to the Harburgh medical facility."

"You know as well as I that once she's admitted there, she'll never come out."

"What's the difference?" He pushed his chair out. "Finishing school or hospital, she'll be gone."

My mouth dropped. Why did it matter to this man? Why was he so determined to help my mother get rid of me?

"The hospital is far less expensive than the school, and she can leave first thing next week. Then you and I ..." his voice trailed off. I could knock Mr. Jonas out if I had the mind to, and I almost did, but I waited until they left our cabin before dressing and racing out the door.

I hadn't planned to speak to Ash-Hair until I'd conquered the ability to catch a squirrel, something I'd been working on during my nightly adventures. I snuck from the house every night and waited until I was deep into the forest to transform. It was much faster to reach Gelid Lake with four legs instead of two. Owls hooted as I passed tree after tree, creating a breeze with my speed that could easily take down a field thistle. I wondered if Cole had returned yet as I remembered the full moon was mere days away, marking the day I'd become sick again if I didn't drink the lake water.

Maybe it'll work if I just drink it tonight and get it over with. I hated being sick.

No, it must be on the night of the full moon, a voice answered back.

Cole, where are you?

He stepped from behind the great sycamore as I skidded to a halt at the edge of the lake. I flicked my tail, not wanting to change back to a human as his facial expression commanded me to do. I snorted, annoyed that this boy could probably talk me into anything with his cold stare.

"Fine," I said, smoothing my dress. "You can't talk to

me as a fox?"

"You've come to feel comfortable in your fur, then?"

"I heard my mother talking about Doc Wilson tonight," I said, getting straight to the point.

"Turns out that poison oak came in handy. Good thinking." He lifted his chin, trying to claim back his pompous ego by acting as if a body rash was the plan the whole time. "I went around telling people Doc Wilson claimed my rashes were crafted by tree gnomes, and I would die in seven days. I said he must have gone mad because it was only a small case of poison oak."

"Well, it worked. You still have a bit there, by the way." I smirked at the rash he tried to hide on his chest under the white shirt.

Cole cleared his throat. "Now that that's taken care of, we need to focus on your ability to perceive a human's intentions – to see if they hold goodness in their heart or hate."

"We can do that?" I waded into the water, wanting to float for a while.

"It's how I was able to determine which prisoners were unjustly captured. I have freed so many innocent people the Shkraykh's food source is becoming scarce."

"So, they're looking for more food, thus your difficulties keeping them contained." I laid my head back, letting the water wash over my cheeks.

"I don't have difficulties," he snapped.

"Boy are you uptight. Why don't you take the night

off from your gloom and doom and come for a swim?" Truth be told, his words made my heart palpitate with anxiety. I needed him to relax so I could.

"You still don't get it, do you? These humans rely on us." He was working himself up again, so I decided to help him cool off. With a wide grin, I brought my arm back and splashed it all over him.

"*Nuh-tahl-ya!*" He broke my name up as he shook the water from his arms.

"So dramatic." I snickered.

I thought he might drown me with the stony stare he was giving me. Instead, he kicked water at me, only hitting me with a few drops. I plodded forward, swinging my arm through the lake to make a wave that soaked the bottom of his black pants. Cole squinted at me as I laughed, then he looked at the sycamore. I didn't know what to say as he pulled off his boots and tunic, then climbed the tree with incredible speed, emerging on a branch high above.

"Oh no." I turned to swim as far as I could. I peered back to see Cole, mid-air, hugging his knees to his chest. He slammed into the water, causing a wave to come crashing over my head. I brought my arms up to cover my face, but it was useless as I was pushed back and under from the impact.

I came up coughing in the center of the lake and wiped my eyes as Cole resurfaced with —

"Are you smiling?" I moved my arms around to keep

myself afloat.

"Nope," he said, looking up, tongue-in-cheek, clearly unable to keep the mirth from his face.

I wanted to say something else, but light caught my attention. Cole and I looked down to see blue orbs surrounding us, tickling our feet. They left the water and floated into the air, circling us like magical little fireflies. I was so entranced with watching them, I only realized they'd been moving us when I smelled sandalwood. I shivered, turning my gaze to see Cole's face close, so close. His smile lessened, though not much, as his eyes searched mine.

He blinked rapidly a few times and ducked under the surface.

"What are you doing?" I asked when he popped up at the edge in fox form. He darted away with no reply.

Why did I care that I hadn't seen Cole in three days?

"He's annoying," I grumbled, taking a swig of water and lacing my boots, readying to go to the lake. The full moon gleamed into my room like a beacon calling for me.

"I'm coming," I snapped at it. I had just retched for the fifth time since the night before, and it became rougher each time – weakening me. My energy was low, not only from the ailment I suffered but hiding my sickness from my mother and Mr. Jonas as I worsened proved to be most tiring.

It was nearing midnight when I left, hobbling through the quiet town. My fox form faltered when running, as well. I was becoming weaker by the moment, and I feared I wouldn't make it to the lake as I toppled into the dirt, my fox voice whimpering in pain. My head turned hot and my vision blurred. I was so tired. Everything seemed so far away. This was it. I wasn't going to make it. Nothing mattered anymore except the pain. I just wanted it to end. I didn't care when the dark figure looming above picked me up. I just wanted the torturous burning behind my ribs to stop.

A miracle trickled down my throat, washing away each jab of pain as it flowed through me. A hand pressed to my dry lips, feeding me the sweetness of Gelid Lake. I was laying, in human form, across Cole's lap.

As the pain subsided and the world came back, embarrassment swept over me. I rolled off of him and knelt beside the sycamore, catching my breath.

"You need to be more careful. If you don't drink the water before midnight, you'll be dead."

"I thought we can't die?" I pushed my hair behind my ears, trying to erase the awkward tension permeating the air.

"I should have been clearer so your brain could process."

I glared at the insult.

"Your human body is not yet fully changed, only

mostly."

"*Mostly* changed?"

He sounded ridiculous.

"Remember when I said you must drink monthly before Feast Day? That day will mark your rebirth as an immortal guardian."

"Next time I'll bring my journal to write down all these rules." I rubbed my temples.

"It's simply common sense."

"Do you ever have anything nice to say?"

"Lover's quarrel?" A girl's voice sounded from the mouth of the forest. Both Cole and I froze. I gasped when I saw Matilda Mae's golden curls bouncing, the moonlight illuminating them in all their perfection.

"Matilda, what are you doing out here?" The overcoming feeling of intimidation never arrived as it would have a month ago when seeing my peers.

"I could ask you the same thing," she said, then cast her enchanting gaze on Cole. "And who is this?"

I inspected his face, not knowing what to do.

"Cole," he said coolly, extending his hand to her. She gave a sweet smile and daintily shook his hand.

"I haven't seen you around before." Matilda straightened her shoulders. I'd known her almost my whole life. I knew she was flirting.

"Cole lives outside of town." I forced my voice to remain calm, even though I wanted to snap.

She twitched her eyebrows at me as if to say, "I'd like

a jab at him."

My protective predator instincts unwillingly kicked in, but I held them steady. "What are you doing here?" I asked again.

"I happened to be coming back from dinner at Charlie's when I saw you stumbling through the street. I thought perhaps you'd had one too many drinks and wanted to check on you."

"Dinner at Charlie's at this time of night?" It wasn't believable. I paused. "You wanted to check on me? Why?"

"Charlie only has his father who works as a logger and is often away." She examined her nails. "I've been watching you, Nathalia. Something's up with you."

"And you want to know my secrets, huh?"

"Just a concerned friend," she said with doe eyes.

"*Friend*?" I was about to unleash the beast. She'd never treated me as a friend.

"I'll escort you ladies home." Cole stood between us and offered both his arms. Matilda wrapped hers around immediately, smiling up at him. I flared my nostrils, wishing she'd go back to Charlie and his stringy yellow hair.

I was nudged, then noticed Cole looking at me, almost signaling for me to take his arm to get her out of there. I held my head high and told myself touching him was just another job to keep a townsperson safe. A nosey, flirtatious, up-to-no-good, townsperson.

"Matilda," Cole addressed her as we came to the town's fence. "I think it's best if we keep this nighttime meeting our secret."

"And we'll keep yours a secret," I said, so quietly that only Cole heard.

"Of course," she said with a side grin, fluttering her lashes. I watched her stare up at him, then immediately regretted it when my skin began to crawl.

"Evening, ladies." Cole nodded at her with a crooked smile like he was flirting back. I stood there, curling my lip, and looking from one to the other. I could have vomited again, but not from my dying body. This sickeningly sweet demeanor of Cole's wasn't his usual, cynical attitude, and it irked me. Why couldn't he be that nice to me?

Matilda watched him walk away, and I smirked to myself, wondering if she'd be so keen on him once she saw him transform into an animal.

"Where have you been hiding *that* boy?" She swung toward me once he'd disappeared through the dark trees.

"I haven't been hiding him."

"So, he's your beau?"

I knew what she was doing, trying to see if he was available. "No. Just a friend."

She grinned with pursed lips and sauntered off through the gates.

"What are you planning, Matilda?" It was a bold question, and she must have thought so too because she looked at me, floored that I'd speak with such a harsh, direct tone.

"I'm not planning *anything*. Just thought he was cute."

"What about Charlie?" I inquired with a raised brow.

"Charlie is … let's just say he won't go much further in life. I'm looking for someone with ambitions and drive."

I could tell her that Cole's entire personality was "drive" – his only mission in life revolved around the Shkraykh. He would *never* look at a girl. "Why don't you focus on *your* ambitions?"

She looked at me like I was crazy, then shook it off. I was glad she walked away, but she turned before I could veer off toward my house. "Want to have lunch tomorrow? My father just got a shipment of German chocolate in, and it's delectable."

"Um …"

"Have you tried German chocolate?"

"No," I said, cautiously.

"Good. It's a date then." Matilda Mae disappeared around a building, leaving me standing under the street lantern, dumbfounded. Other emotions I couldn't identify stirred within me as I inspected the forest, quiet and still, knowing a silver fox lurked somewhere out there, and I couldn't help but wonder if what he *thought* was his purpose was truly enough for him.

Chapter Seven
Goodbye

"I told Charlie I was in search of something more, to find my true self, and he should do the same." Matilda had spoken endlessly for the past hour. She popped a grape in her mouth as we sat at her mahogany kitchen table perched on a shiny wooden floor, a house only the rich could afford. "He was upset, of course, but I told him I needed someone with dreams as big as mine."

"And what are your newfound dreams, Matilda?" I was truly curious, seeing as how it'd only been eleven hours since we had that enlightening talk.

"I'll move to Harburgh, in the middle of the city, and become an actress. My face will be on pamphlets and in the newspaper. I can sing and dance." Her eyes were glued to the ceiling in a dreamy way, like she was envisioning herself on stage.

"That's a beautiful dream, Matilda." There wasn't an ounce of dishonesty in my words.

She was eccentric, but I could tell from sitting and talking with her that she wasn't the vapid girl I thought she was. She just needed to know the option to be destined for greatness was available. I fidgeted with my hands, remembering Cole telling me the same thing – I wasn't simple-minded like Charlie and his cronies thought.

I decided at that moment I would dedicate myself to my new life as Cole had – to *really* focus, to stop ignoring the main purpose, which was a battle between good and evil. I wasn't positive I could do it, but for once in my life, I wanted to face the fear.

"Where are you going?" Matilda asked as I stood.

"I have something to do, but maybe we can do this again soon? You can tell me about your love for the theater."

I'd never seen the brown-eyed, platinum-blonde beauty smile in such a childish way. It was excitement, like her eight-year-old self was cheering her for finally realizing what she was meant to become.

After I left, I walked straight to Gelid Lake. I didn't change into an animal, but slowly, taking in all the sights and sounds as a human. What would it be like when I'm "reborn" as an immortal? I could only assume my senses would become equal to the silver fox's. I strolled away from the path, noticing the small wildlife that would be my only food source within the year. I stopped to gaze at a bird's nest, smiling at the tiny mouths peeping out from it. I touched the tree bark and the leaves. I never truly appreciated my humanity, and, though I was ready to take on my forever future, I would mourn this Nathalia when she was gone.

I was glad Cole wasn't at the lake. I wanted to sit alone with my thoughts in the presence of the sprites who gave me this opportunity. With each full moon that would pass, I'd fall further and further from my human self, so I sat with my feet in the water, and said goodbye to myself. A bittersweet farewell.

Hours had gone by, but I was at peace. The sprites whirled about me, dancing around my ankles and toes, and I could tell they were happy.

"Is this what you spend your time doing?"

I lunged forward, letting out a scream and nearly falling into the lake. "Cole," I clutched my chest. "Is it your plan to kill me with a heart attack before I become immortal?"

"I didn't think I was that hideous." With hands in his pockets, he leaned his back against the tree. "Your friend seemed to think just the opposite." He smirked.

"Don't even think about it," I warned. I removed my feet from the water and wiped my hands as I stood. "I'm ready."

"For what, exactly?"

"This. All of it. I can catch rodents and fish, but I want to learn something challenging. So, what do you have for me?"

His face dropped like he never thought I'd become serious in a million years.

"Well?" I asked.

"Alright then." He smiled, just barely, and led me to a field where deer frequented. He gave me instructions as we transformed into our silver-furred bodies. Cole taught me to pounce, and how to silently creep toward the prey as we waited for dusk to hit.

· ——❉—— ·

"Ya did good, kid," he said after a successful hunt, although he didn't eat.

"Thank you, darling," I teased, tying my hair back. Going from animal to human ruffled my appearance. "What now?"

"Sleep. Get home before you get into trouble."

"I don't want to go home yet."

"Why not?" He was already walking away and didn't seem too interested in my answer.

"My mother … well, she's planning on sending me to the hospital in Harburgh."

Cole turned, eyes narrowed with concern. "If you go in there …"

"I'll never come out," I finished.

"What about your father? Does he feel the same?"

"Pa disappeared twelve years ago." I swallowed.

"I'm more of a rock in Ma's shoe than anything."

Was it sympathy I saw on Cole's face?

"I overheard her say she's sending me next week."

He licked his lips and pressed them together. His eyes flickered back and forth as the wheels in his brain turned. "They'll have you board the train, no doubt," he said after a minute. I nodded. "I'll follow it until its next stop. Then you'll sneak off, and they'll never know."

"You don't think they'll have an escort for me?" I asked.

"I'll take care of that. Don't worry. Now go." Cole left and I found myself desperately wishing he didn't. I went back to the cabin and stared at it before going inside. It wasn't home. It never really had been.

"Nathalia!" my mother screamed from the kitchen, though my small bedroom was directly connected to it.

"Coming." I left my room with my one bag of belongings, my stomach turning at the uncertainty of what the day would bring. Cole hadn't been around since I told him I was leaving, so I didn't know what the exact plan was.

"Put that by the door," she said, fastening her bonnet. I peeked into her bedroom and saw three suitcases sitting on the bed. It was clear she was leaving and had no intention of returning.

"I'm not sick," I said, meekly. I dared to touch her arm, one last attempt to see if she could find any love for me at all.

"You *are* sick." She sighed, flinching at my cold touch and shrugging me off. "You'll be better off."

I could almost see a hint of something in her eyes … whether regret, sympathy, or shame, I didn't know, but it certainly wasn't love.

A knock came at the door.

"Good morning, ma'am." Cole, dressed in a medical uniform, stood at our front door. I wanted to laugh, forgetting my mother's harsh demeanor a second ago.

"Tell the station clerk you're meeting Mr. Sacron on platform three." She shoved an envelope into Cole's hands. "When you find him, let him know he'll find the payment information inside. Do *not* lose this, boy." She turned to me. "You'll be better off," she said to my face. I took my bag and walked out without so much as a goodbye.

"Cole, stop clutching my arm so tight," I whispered as we walked.

"Just playing the part." He eased up, but I could tell he was enjoying this. I glanced over my shoulder to see Ma standing in the doorframe. Her expression was cold, but her eyes … I couldn't tell. I didn't even try to hide my anguish as I turned back to the road.

Cole helped me into the cart that was to take us to the train station and climbed up after me. "Don't look back."

It was good advice, and I knew he meant it metaphorically, too. I watched the trees go by, and the small-town buildings, and the townsfolk who, for the most part, had never shown me a bit of kindness.

"I could have helped you down," Cole said after I jumped from the carriage. It was a three-hour ride to the station, and my legs were restless. The train platform was bustling with people as we made our way through. I tripped on an uneven board, nearly knocking over a man in a fancy suit, and he didn't seem too thrilled.

"My apologies, sir. My wife has had a bit too much to drink," Cole said to the man.

My mouth dropped as the man glared at me in disgust and walked on.

"*Cole!*"

He obviously found himself amusing, judging by the sound of his idiotic cackling. "Down here," he said, motioning toward a small staircase after seeing a medical-looking man whom we could only assume was Mr. Sacron.

We descended the stairs leading away from the platform and train and distanced ourselves from the sound of voices and the train whistle as we made our way to the quiet woods. We walked further and further in until the smoke from the station was like a freshly extinguished candle.

Cole reached behind a log and pulled out a bundle of clothing.

"I think your new look suits you." I gave him a large, fake smile as he huffed and tossed me a dress. I couldn't find anything to make fun of as I ran my hand down the silk fabric, finer than any dress I'd ever owned. The blue was like the night sky illuminated by the moon, appropriate for someone like me. *A creature of the night.*

"Where did you get this," I exhaled.

"I had to go into the city to get these." He pulled at the scruff of the medical shirt. "I thought I might as well grab you something."

I watched his eyes before he turned his back to me and removed the clinical shirt to replace it with his usual white shirt and leather tunic. I gawked at the blemished skin on his back. Scars covered him. Bite marks and scratches and deeper cuts were scattered around. He finished dressing and fastened the belt, adjusting it when he turned and saw me staring.

"Well, change," he ordered.

"Here?" My cheeks burned. There was no way I was undressing in the middle of the woods and in front of him.

"Nathalia, I'm not going to look. I'm not interested in looking, trust me."

While I thought he was rude and annoying, those words jabbed at me. Of course, I wouldn't want his eyes on me as I changed, but boy did he make it clear I wasn't even tempting. He sat on a log and pulled off his shoes, replacing them with brown leather boots, not looking my way. As quickly as I could, I swapped my simple dress for the gown. I examined the sleeves that clung to my elbow and placed my hand over the silver neckline. This is what Ma wanted – a million of these.

"Take down your hair."

I looked up to see Cole's icy eyes glued to me. His expression made me feel like one of the pretty girls, though apparently I "wasn't tempting" to him. I took out my braid, letting the wavy, brown hair fall on my shoulders. The breath caught in my throat as he walked to me and carefully ran his fingers down a strand of my hair, smoothing the small knots out.

"Messy hair isn't refined." He said it like he had to make an excuse for why his hand had lingered in my hair. "Let's go." He stared for a moment more, then walked past me, back toward the station.

"We're going back?"

"Unless you'd like to walk miles upon miles back to the lake?"

I joined him and we, again, walked the station platform. Mr. Sacron examined his watch, then looked around, impatient and annoyed.

Cole pulled my arm as I veered toward a small carriage. "This one."

"*That* one?" The most beautiful black coach sat before

us, trimmed in gold and taller than two horses stacked together.

"To Ward's Crossing," Cole said, placing a small bag of coins into the driver's hand. I waited until we were in the coach to ask where on Earth he got that much money.

"When you have all the time in the world, you find ways to earn side cash." He shrugged and looked out the window. I knew now why I had to change into such a lavish gown. We had to look rich enough to afford this, and Mr. Sacron wouldn't give us a second look.

"Thank you," I said, an hour into the quiet trip. "For coming up with this plan."

"I didn't have much of a choice. You'd die in the hospital, and I'd have to answer to the sprites." He was putting up a cold front again, so I stopped talking. The coach dropped us at the crossroads, and after he drove the horses away, Cole and I walked the opposite direction of Moss Grove.

I changed back into my regular dress behind the sycamore once we'd reached the lake.

"I don't want to ruin it," I said, folding it and gently pushing it into my carpet luggage bag.

"Here." Cole handed me an envelope.

"What's this?" I unfolded the paper.

"The deed to your mother's house."

I nearly dropped the paper as I gawked at him.

"I found out she was selling it, so I bought it. You don't need a lot of sleep or food, and you won't be cold in the winter, but I thought you'd want a familiar place to stay, since you're new to this life and all."

"I … oh I could just kiss you right now!" *I didn't mean to say that, oh my gosh.*

"A 'thank you' will suffice." He turned away from me to stare at the lake. I didn't know what else to say, but I had to move away from him so he wouldn't see my beat-red face. I picked up a stone and tossed it at the lake, attempting to steady my breath.

What a stupid, stupid thing to say. I skipped another. *Idiot!*

"You call that skipping a rock?" Cole said. "Let me show you how it's done." He picked up a large, smooth stone and chucked it. It bounced delicately across seven times.

"Show-off."

The early autumn breeze brushed my hair to the side.

"I'm not surprised you're no good."

I swung to him. "Why, because I'm a girl?"

"Oh, no—" His face tightened with worry for a moment, like insulting me was the last thing he wanted to do, then it fell into a sly side smirk. "I very much like girls."

I rolled my eyes and threw another rock. "Alright, Romeo. When was the last time you took a girl out?"

He didn't reply, but still held his foolish expression. "You should go home and unpack," Cole said after our quip bantering faded. I bit my bottom lip, my mind reverting back to the deed of my house. The suitcases on Ma's bed, selling the house … she left and I knew she had no intention of returning. She thought I was locked up for good, no longer her burden. But the house was mine. Completely my own.

I nodded slowly and picked up my bag.

I lit a candle and walked around the cabin, running my hand over the fireplace. I sat on Ma's bed, feeling my throat swell. I laid down on the pillows and blankets she'd left behind and cried until the sun set.

I would forget most of my troubles when I was with Cole. He was a decent distraction, but when I was alone again, the hurt overcame me. I had never imagined getting married – I was too plain looking and "adventurous" to be a wife, but I'd have to cut off all contact with everyone. Was Cole to be my only friend for the rest of my life? Anyone else would see that I don't age, and who knew what would happen then? Just more heartbreak for me.

Chapter Eight
Don't Fall

I washed in the water basin and decided to go for a run, wanting to practice so Cole wouldn't have any snide comments when the time came for testing my agility.

I was approaching the gates when I saw a familiar face.

"What the heck are you doing here?" I asked Cole when I saw him in front of the inn, a bouquet of flowers in hand.

"Waiting for my date."

"Your what, now?"

"I thought I'd resurrect my charm, so I'm escorting Matilda to a lush dinner." He puffed out his chest, standing up straighter and looking proud of himself.

"Cole, that's weird. You're two hundred years old."

"Correction, I have been eighteen for two hundred years."

I crossed my arms. "It's still weird."

"Shush, here she comes." He walked past me to greet Matilda. I couldn't hear what he said to her, but she giggled and smelled the flowers. He offered his arm and they entered the inn.

"I don't care. I don't care," I told myself as I jogged away from the inn.

I raced throughout the night, weaving through the forest, even jumping over bushes like I was in an obstacle course. I pushed myself to keep going, slowing to catch my breath but never stopping, knowing that Feast Day would be an all-night event, and I needed the stamina.

I dashed to the lake, pouncing into it and lapping it up to cool myself down. When I reached the other side of the deep, dark lake, I shook my silver fur and noticed I was standing at the edge of the forest that led to the gorge. I took in a breath and grew, losing the fur and snout. Back on two legs, I ventured forward.

I need to face it, I thought. *I'll show him how tough I can be.*

The affirmation was only that. Instead, my confidence to become brave wavered as the cliffs came into view. The waning gibbous moon shone light upon the streamers of death. I shivered from the sight of the few remaining mangled bodies the Shkraykh hadn't finished. I wanted to leave, to run far from the grim smell of rot, but I stayed, swallowing the bile in my throat. I needed to adjust to the death.

I inched closer to the edge, peering down. If I climbed into the gorge, I could get a better look at the human remains. Cole had told me we had an intuition, that we could sense what was in a human's heart. I wondered if it worked for the deceased.

There's a spot, I thought, spying a piece of rock jutting out. My boot knocked pebbles from the ledge as I lowered myself down, my part-human heart beating wildly. With my feet planted firmly on the stone, I clutched the upper ledge, peering over my shoulder at the drop. This was much different than climbing trees. I scaled the length of the ledge, treading carefully, to another flat rock below. Again, I slid down to it, grateful this one was a few inches wider than the other.

Two down, a thousand more to go. I slid my feet toward the other side when I felt my dress being pulled. I gasped and glanced over to see a small, brown, prickle bush growing under the upper ledge. I hadn't noticed it, but it attempted to take my dress as its own.

"Perfect," I stated with an exasperated sigh. With one hand firm on a small bump on the cliff wall, I tugged at the fabric. "Come on," I growled, pulling harder. With one more swift yank, it was free, but I lost my grip and my footing. I swung my arms out, trying to regain balance and catch a grip on the ledge, but it was no use. My body tilted backward. Would I die if I wasn't fully immortal? Was I about to lay smashed on the ravine floor below?

The thought blew through my mind, and I closed my eyes, fear striking like lightning, when a pair of hands grabbed my waist and pulled me forward. My body pressed into theirs as they tightened their grip around my lower back. I opened my eyes to see Cole with his back against the wall.

"Get on," he said, but when I gave him a frightened, blank stare, he continued, "Put your arms around my neck and hold on."

I did as he said, not daring to consider the other option. Cole lifted me up without warning, wrapping my legs around his waist. I screamed as he jumped from the ledge and landed on a tree branch growing from a crack in a lower rock. I tucked my face into his shoulder and squeezed my eyes shut while Cole rapidly climbed the cliff with ease.

"Okay," he breathed, winded. "You're safe."

I didn't move, except for my uncontrollable shaking.

"Nathalia, you can get down now," he said, holding his arms out to the side as I clung to him like a sloth. I dropped, my trembling legs landing on firm ground, and swallowed, seeing that we were somehow back at Gelid Lake.

"How did you do that?" I marveled, remembering how fast he'd climbed the sycamore.

"Are you crazy?" He reamed into me. "Why would you ever try to climb down there, especially since you aren't a full immortal!" He ran his fingers through his hair and continued. "Are you trying to die?"

That answered my question about the result of the fall. "I was trying to tap into that intuition thing you told me about."

He licked his teeth and huffed out an exasperated laugh, while his white eyes bore into me. "With a corpse?" he finally asked. "You really are crazy. Once they're dead, it's over. There's no soul left inside for you to inspect."

"Well, if you would tell me these things, I wouldn't have ventured down there!"

"No, you ventured down to prove yourself to me."

"I did *not!*" I did.

"If we're talking about intuition, let me enlighten you." Cole took a step toward me, standing three inches away, and his sandalwood smell enveloped me. "I can read you like a book."

I blushed, now knowing he could tell how unsettled I was at this close proximity.

"You're a naive little girl, Nathalia. If it wasn't for me, you'd be dead." He turned away for a second, then whipped back around to continue insulting me. "You know, if you *had* fallen to your death, you'd have messed up the sprites' plans. If I can't hold the Shkraykh back because you decided to have yourself an adventure, innocent human blood would have been on your hands."

I threw up my hands, affronted. "Why don't you pull the stick out of your butt, Cole?"

The fury in his eyes was no match for what was boiling inside me. My eyes watered, but not because my feelings were hurt.

I was seething.

"Aren't you supposed to be my mentor or something? But instead of mentoring, you disappear for days, then yell at me for not magically knowing the stupid rules. So no, the blood won't be on my hands, Cole. It'll be on yours!" I darted away before the influx of tears rolled down my cheeks.

I figured I wouldn't see him for a few days while he licked his wounds, so I would use that time to study the gorge. Was there an entrance to the bottom where Cole stood guard on Feast Day?

If he won't teach me, I'll take matters into my own hands.

"Hi, Matilda," I said the next morning after entering the general store, still a bit red in the face.

"Oh," she said rather unenthusiastically. "Hello." She didn't sound thrilled to see me, a much different attitude than when we had lunch.

Matilda watched me pick up a pair of binoculars. I figured I could use them to see if the other side of the cliff had an easier way to the bottom.

"Bird watching." I gave her a soft smile, hoping she wouldn't start talking about how weird I was. What girl buys binoculars? Not many around here. "Is something wrong?" I asked after she gave me a look of wild disapproval.

74

"You told me he wasn't your beau," she said, slipping her hand into a new pair of lace gloves.

"Who, Cole? He certainly isn't."

"You might want to tell him that." She examined her dainty hand, then faced me. "I don't know why he'd ask me on a date if he was just going to talk about you the whole time."

I raised a brow. "What did he say?"

He could only have complained the whole time, surely.

Matilda pulled off the gloves and set them on the counter, paid the cashier, then stuffed them in her purse. She secured a curl behind her ear. "I hope to find someone who talks about me the way Cole does about you when I'm in the big city." She gave me a small, serene smile, and left.

I lost my ability to breathe and move. What could she mean, alluding to Cole speaking about me in a positive way?

"Young, Miss Richards." The deep, grating voice came from close behind me, and I turned to see —

"Doc Wilson." I gulped, relaxing my face so he wouldn't notice my unease.

"You're looking …" He looked me up and down. "… healthier."

"I'm fantastic. Never felt more alive." My choice of words probably wasn't the most fitting, but I kept my confidence and gave him a smile. I had to throw the doctor off our trail.

The store's bell jingled when two women stepped in, immediately sharing whispers as they eyed Wilson. I held back a grin, knowing this meant Cole's rumors truly did work. The doctor squinted at me, then tipped his hat and left.

"Miss Richards," one of the women said. "We thought you and your mother had left town."

Oh no, I didn't think about that part. "My mother did. She told me to stay put until she found us a place to live. She didn't want to move me from inn to inn."

The woman raised a brow and made a small click with her tongue, and the two continued with their shopping. I paid for the binoculars and departed the store, glancing around before sneaking into the woods.

I love this, I thought while my paws gently kicked up dirt. I could go faster than any horse. I was light, agile, and if I fell … well I was closer to the ground than my five-foot, five-inch human body. I dropped the satchel I'd secured around my long body and transformed.

Scanning the gorge floor was much easier with binoculars.

Stairs, or a cave entrance that leads above, maybe? The dry, mostly dead area had no noise but there was a breeze blowing up dust, and the sound of vultures. My senses were becoming stronger, but I didn't hear the footsteps behind me. A bag was pulled over my head and forceful-gripping hands pinned my arms to my side so I couldn't move. I kicked out, trying to free myself, but someone grabbed my legs and bound my feet. I screamed, but it was muffled by the thick, burlap fabric. They carried me as I struggled and dropped me onto a hard platform – a cart, I soon realized, as I was jolted around when the horse was commanded forward.

"Did you bind her properly, Wilson?"

No, NO. I grunted, but I couldn't yell through the fabric adhered to my mouth. I could barely breathe as it was. I lay still and tried to think. Maybe Cole should have killed Doc Wilson and fed him to the Shkraykh. Maybe I will when I get out of here.

I focused, calming myself to transform, hoping the rope tied tightly around my ankles and wrists would be too large for paws. I took in air and let it out, trying to ignore the strings from the sack that landed on my tongue. I stilled my body and focused.

"Oh no you don't," Wilson raged.

I faded to black, feeling the blood drip from my head, wondering if what he hit me with was strong enough to kill a part-immortal.

Chapter Nine
Vastaya

"She's a Cold One, I'm sure of it."

My enhanced hearing caught the conversation outside the room I laid in – the room I was confined to – bound with rubber straps and a skinny tube embedded in my wrist, pushing liquid into my veins. My mouth was bitterly dry, and my head pounded. I tried to swallow, but I had no saliva. I slowly glanced around, trying to adjust my hazy eyes.

It was no doctor's office. Not a hospital, or even a room at an inn. Everything was white - the walls, the floor, the tiny bed that wasn't much wider than my body. Panic nearly overtook me, but I fought it. Whatever the men were saying outside was important.

"We'll give you one month, Wilson, but if she doesn't carry the symptoms, you'll be finished."

Multiple pairs of boots sounded on the floor, walking away from the room. Doc Wilson entered. His expression held a type of worried determination, until he saw I was awake. It immediately relaxed to a satisfied and conniving look.

"Well, you've been out for quite some time. It's funny, you didn't seem to need any nourishment for the past few days."

A few days!

"How many?" was my question instead of *why are you doing this?* My voice came out as a croaked whisper.

"Four. Very impressive." He stuck me with a needle, drawing blood from my veins, and I winced as he inserted it into a tube.

"What are you doing with that?" I wiggled, trying to loosen the constraints.

"Don't bother struggling; it's useless." Wilson labeled the little bottle and plucked out a strand of my hair.

"What's that for?" I could feel the heat in my body rising when he ignored me again. "Doctor Wilson, you know me, you've been our doctor since we moved to Moss Grove. Why—"

He shushed me like a father soothing his child. "This is much bigger than formalities, young Nathalia. Your fox lover has created a monstrosity that must be cleansed. Tell me where he is."

"I don't know." It was the truth. I didn't know where Cole lived. Did he have a place somewhere? Or did he live in a burrow as a fox?

"Don't lie to me," Wilson growled.

This man was not the one I knew. He was the opposite. Doc Wilson was a persona, a mask. He'd been searching for the Cold One his entire life. These symptoms his colleagues spoke of …

That's why he became a doctor in the first place, I gathered within the few seconds I inspected his expression. His very nature permeated the room, smelling as foul as his intentions. The instincts Cole spoke of … was I tapping into them?

What are the symptoms? No pulse, no heartbeat, and chilled, pale skin. What else?

What did Cole have that I didn't? I wasn't fully immortal, of course, but he was just as cold as I – just as pale, too.

Maybe pessimism is a symptom.

I couldn't suppress my laughter at the thought. How could I possibly joke at a time like this? Wilson slapped my face so hard I tasted the blood.

"Are you a loony, girl? You must be – laughing about such matters."

"One is standing in this room, but it's not me," I spat, wondering where my audacity came from. He raised a hand to strike me again, but I held my gaze on his eyes. He lowered his hand and let out a deep chuckle.

"Bravery." Wilson reached into his pocket and removed a small, leather notebook with a pen attached by a ribbon and scribbled something.

A symptom?

"Your mother must be worried. Do not fret, young lady. We'll get you better in no time." His grin was wicked and collusive. My stomach turned when he took the tube connected to my wrist and secured it to a new bag filled with thick, silver liquid before he exited the room. I was utterly alone.

I slept unwillingly, waking in the same spot – tied down like an animal.

An animal!

Focus, I told myself. No one was in the room, giving me time to transform. I'd bite Wilson's face off the moment he stepped through the door. I slowed my mind and envisioned myself shrinking, slipping off the straps binding me, leaping from the bed to hide behind the door, waiting for the attack, but my skin burned. I cried out as a pure-white rash appeared on parts of my skin.

The doctor entered and laughed. "The Luminary won't doubt me, now," he exclaimed, clapping at the sight.

"What did you do to me, you monster," I bellowed.

"I, the monster? No, girl. You are, but I mourn for you."

I ground my teeth.

"The Cold One did this to you, and he will pay for his crimes. But you are beyond saving, I'm afraid."

More white spots terrorized my skin as I attempted to transform again.

"You're only hurting yourself, young lady. See that?" He pointed to the tube of silver. "That's an extract from a flower called Midnight Nerium. It's an uncommon variant of Dogbane." He flicked the bag, making it drip faster. "It's harmful to dogs. Did you know a fox is part of the canid family, Nathalia?"

Oh God, he's killing me.

"I'm glad to see it's working. It will be impossible for you to mutate while this is in your system. You'll only hurt yourself if you try. There will be time for you to show your abilities soon." Wilson hiked up his brown pants and pulled up a seat next to my bed. He pushed his glasses up his nose. "Now," he said, scratching something down in his notebook. "What do you know about the Shkraykh?"

Like I'd tell you. "Nothing, other than they feast on the corpses of prisoners and innocent men, if given the chance."

"Is that all?" he inquired, his voice hinting at his disbelief.

"I haven't been told anything else."

Wilson squinted, then scribbled some more notes. I tried leaning my head over to see, but my arms were bound so tightly to my side, I couldn't move more than an inch.

"How about the silver fox? Where does he hide?"

"No idea."

"Nathalia, if you work with me, we can ease the

suffering the Cold One has caused."

"You're the cause of my pain right now!"

He shook his head and wrote something down. "It will only get worse from here, but if you insist on being difficult, you leave me no choice." He put the notebook and pencil in his briefcase, flicked the dripping bag again, and left me there in agony. Tears ran down the side of my face and into my hair as I tried to come up with an escape plan.

Wilson rubbed his chin as he considered my words. He'd left me there for another day in misery, but when he finally entered the room, I pleaded with him in desperate sobs.

"I don't want to be a monster, please help me! I want to go home now, please," I cried out. My overflow of tears was genuine, so was my desperate begging to go home.

"How long have you been plagued, Nathalia?" His demeanor flipped, his good, wholesome, family doctor facade in action once again, as he approached my bed.

"A month," I said, truthfully, whimpering for dramatics.

"Not long." There was a sort of hope in his eyes ... hope for what, I didn't know, but it certainly wasn't for saving my life.

"We must run tests, but I warn you, they can be brutal."

"But why?" I complained, trying to sound as young and innocent as possible.

"We must know how this disease works. Over many years we have gathered information on the Cold One. Tales of a boy who fell into a lake and, shortly after, lost his pulse, his color, and his heartbeat. He became aggressive, terrifying people." He closed his notebook. "Alright, young lady. I will allow you the opportunity to help us." He cut the rubber and removed the syringe, to my immense relief. He helped me out of the bed. I was weak, my legs wobbly, but it wasn't as bad as it would have been if I were full human.

"What are you doing?" I asked as he tied my wrists behind my back with more rubber rope.

"I can't take any chances of aggression. You understand." Wilson walked me to a metal door that had been outside my field of vision when I was lying on the bed. There were at least fifteen latches down it.

"This room will be more comfortable as we attempt to expel the devil within you."

Inside was another white room, empty except for a bed.

"Please ..." I cried. "Can't I go home? You can come with me and study me there! I swear I'll do anything and everything you ask."

It was a longshot, I knew. But I was desperate.

"Nathalia," he said, placing a hand on my shoulder. "I know you would never lash out on purpose, but we must take precaution. As long as you prove yourself, you will no longer suffer the effects of the Midnight Nerium."

He stepped out of the room and closed the door. I heard all fifteen locks click before I climbed into the bed, not knowing how long the poison would flow through my veins. The rashes were fading, my body healing quickly, but I still cried. Not because I was sad, I was trapped here, but tears of anger.

I drifted off into the abyss, and where I landed was no dream. My intuition sensed it. I felt the warmth of the air. I smelled rosemary, thyme, and lavender – so many sweet smells, but I could separate each one on its own.

"Nathalia," a chorus sang out in unison. A wonderful array of lights formed as women glided to me with their arms stretched out, bringing the clearing and the lake into view.

"Who are you?" I asked, not a feeling of fear within me.

"We are the sprites, child."

My mouth opened in awe as they came into view – angelic creatures clad in the purest of white dresses and flowers weaved throughout their soft hair.

"You're not little balls of light with webbed feet and water wings," I exclaimed.

Their laughs were otherworldly, like bells in Heaven. "No, child. This is our astral form. Observe yourself."

The one in the front brought her arm up, directing my attention to Gelid Lake, clear as polished glass. I peered into the surface at my reflection. My face seemed different, just barely, but I couldn't put my finger on it. My eyes were still cucumber-green, my nose still had no freckles, which I'd always been disappointed about, and my lips were as thin as ever. No, I looked no different.

"Do you know where you are?" the sprite asked.

"In a dream, I suppose." I was sick and my mind was feeble. Maybe my intuition was wrong about it not being a dream. Because I knew I was really being held in a white room, somewhere hidden.

"You are not, my dear. You've tapped into something – an ability that took the silver fox a full year to master."

My breath quickened. "Did I escape? Can I disappear from one spot and end up in another?"

"Not your body, but your mind, yes." She approached me. "This is your astral body."

"But I can feel this." I ran my hand through the soft grass.

"Your astral body is not like your dream body. It is one entirely different; one that has access to all the senses and more."

"Am I in another world?"

"You are in Vastaya. This is our safe haven. It is yours now, as well," another sprite spoke.

"The cursed land? How?" I took in the sight – the full trees, the moss – so cushioned one could use it as a bed. It was the same clearing, but prettier somehow.

"We knew man would discover it on Earth one day, so we preserved it forever in this realm."

"May I ask you something?" I didn't know if I should, if it was appropriate, but wanted to know the answer anyway. "Why did you choose me?"

The sprite lowered her head and softened her features more than they already were. "You are pure of heart, child. You are inquisitive and see life as it should be in the details of our world. You are sensitive and kind."

"I'm sensitive, but that makes me weak. I cry too much, and I get so angry," I said, knowing I couldn't be pure in heart.

Again, they laughed like angels. "We all get angry, Nathalia. It's what you are angry for, and how you choose to react after making a mistake that makes you pure. Your sensitivity is not a weakness, no matter how many tears you shed. You *feel* to your very core, and that, my child is strength." A bird darted down and landed on the sprite's dark, outstretched hand. She stroked its back while she talked. "You must release yourself from the prison in which you are held. We need you. Humanity needs you." She settled a meaningful look at me. "*Cole* needs you."

"Cole has expressed many times he doesn't, that he can do it on his own." I thought back to Matilda and her words, wondering just what nice things he could have possibly said about me.

"He is a foolish boy, stuck in his ways." She grinned, and I could tell she loved him like a son.

"We knew the moment you touched our tree you were good for him." A different sprite stepped forward.

I'd die of shock if he ever uttered the word, "help."

"How do I get away from the doctor?" I asked.

"It is a task you must figure out."

"To prove I'm strong enough for the Shkraykh? Did you do this to me as a test?" I felt anger rising in my chest until the first sprite placed a cool hand on my shoulder.

"No, Nathalia. We," she motioned to the group, "are bound to the lake. We would never put you in such a situation. You are now our child; we are your mothers.

"I'm sorry." The stupid tears rose in my eyes.

"You can do this. A fox's instincts are sly, and they are fantastic problem solvers."

I had wondered why they chose a fox form for us, but I never asked.

"We have the utmost faith in you, and should you need help, you'll know where to look." She kissed my cheek. Then one by one, the others followed suit, their lips nourishing me and giving me mindful strength. I didn't want them to go, just as I didn't want to leave such a perfect, peaceful, safe place.

I have twenty-four days. I can stay in this paradise a little longer, I thought, and moved to the moss bed, inhaling the scent of nature.

What the sprite said about Cole wouldn't leave my mind. "You are good for Cole."

I wondered where he was, and if he noticed or cared I'd gone missing at all.

Chapter Ten
Only a Week

Hours passed in the astral realm ... I think. I hadn't grown tired as I thought I would when the sprites left, though I enjoyed laying in the moss. I drank from the lake, savoring every drop of sumptuous water. I spun through the fields in bliss, never wanting to feel my human body again.

"They told me I'd find you here."

I turned in surprise, but a giddy smile spread across my face as I sauntered forward. "I haven't seen you in a while, Cole."

"What's wrong with you?"

"What's wrong with *you*? How can you still be a sourpuss in such a marvelous place?" My giggle was preposterous as I poked his shoulder.

"Oh no," he groaned. "How long have you been here, Nathalia?"

"Just a few hours."

He twitched his brow like he didn't believe me.

"Come on, you have to taste the clovers." I snatched

his hand and pulled him along as I skipped to a patch filled entirely with four-leaf clovers. I popped one in my mouth, savoring the sweetness. "Mmmm. Here," I said, nearly shoving it in his face, which was painted with surprise.

"Go on." I trailed it across his cheek and across his lips, which finally parted. He ate the savory treat, not removing his narrowed eyes from mine. The vegetation in Vastaya was nothing like anything I'd ever tasted. It was indescribable. The sprites said I had all of my senses "and more." I'd assumed I was able to have the pleasure of enjoying every fiber of nature like no one else could.

"Delicious," he said in a flat tone. "Okay, time to go."

I gasped and clapped my hands together. "We should skip rocks!" Again, I brought him, staggering behind me, to the fatter part of the lake. "They're all flat. It's like the sprites knew I'd love them."

"Nathalia," he began, but I interrupted.

"Are you afraid I've become better than you? I have been practicing," I gloated. He bit the inside of his cheek and considered, then shook his head in defeat and grabbed up a stone, flicking it ten times across the water.

"Hm," I said in a sly tone and skipped my rock fifteen times. His mouth dropped and his brow knit.

"Told you so." I flipped my hair over my shoulder.

Cole's appearance turned stern again. "Nathalia, it's time to go, now."

"You drive me nuts," I groaned, never wanting to

leave.

"You *are* a nut."

I knocked him to the ground, pinning down his arms, sitting over him, and he snorted out a surprised laugh.

"Have you ever heard the saying, 'boys go to Jupiter to get more stupider'?"

"That's the dumbest expression I've ever heard. Get off, kid!"

"Not until you admit it."

"Admit what?" He wiggled under my unusually strong grip.

"That I'm better at skipping rocks than you."

"Ha!"

"Say it," I demanded, leaning closer to him. When he didn't answer, I tickled his side and wouldn't let up.

"Alright, alright," he gasped through a wide smile, then he flipped me over, pinning me to the ground.

"Nathalia, you're proficient in rock skipping. A pure master." His dramatic tone amused me.

He released my arms, and I patted his cheek. "Thank you, precious."

"Yeah, yeah. You know for a thistle, you're pretty thorny."

"Maybe I'm finally a rose." I twitched my brow and pushed off the ground. "What should we do now? Race? I can jump at least five —"

"*Nathalia*," he stated. "You have to return, now. Staying in Vastaya for so long is … well, it can alter your mind."

"I've never felt better." I took both of his hands and pulled him to me. "Wanna roll down that hill?"

His eyes saddened, and he removed his hands from mine, then wrapped them around my arms. "Vastaya is a beautiful escape, a vacation of sorts. But if we stay for too long, we'll be lost."

"Are you that much of a fun sucker, Cole?"

"Do you want to die? Do you want me to die? How about innocent men, women, and even children? They'll all be wiped out if you don't finish your treatments." His white eyes and ash hair became vibrant, the sun giving his light skin a sort of shimmer.

My eyes darted around me at the perfection of where I stood, the illusion of it all crashing down. Death, that's all there would be if I didn't get out of … wherever I was.

"I understand you're upset with me, but that doesn't give you the right to abandon your post," he said sternly. "Not when there's still much training to be done, and with the full moon only a week away —"

"A week?" I blinked, frantic and confused. "No, that can't be right. I've only been gone for five, maybe six days. I have plenty of time to return."

"Well, I haven't seen you around, and you were beyond euphoric a moment ago, which tells me you've been here for a while." Cole removed his hands from my arms. "I'm surprised you were able to tap into your astral body so soon," he admitted.

"I'm stuck somewhere." I gazed about the field, ignoring him.

"We're in Vastaya, the way it was before it was disturbed by the witches. The sprites kept it for us all to heal when we needed to. It's how we stay alive, in a way." He, again, gripped my hand gently. "You need to return, Nathalia, do you understand? And if I find you famished and dying in the woods again because you were irresponsible getting to the lake in time, I'll dunk your head in the water until you're a full immortal."

I couldn't believe the smirk across his face ... that what he said wasn't genuine anger or annoyance. His words were playful, fun. So unlike him.

"Doc Wilson abducted me," I shot out, remembering exactly what happened. "I don't know where I am." Tears threatened to burst from my eyes, but I pushed them away with my determination to escape.

Cole clutched my cold hands and stared blankly into the field just past my head, like he was having a vision. "Wherever you are, it's well hidden." He fixed his eyes on mine. "What did you notice around you? What have you seen?"

He still held my hands, but I didn't pull away. I needed the comfort, even if it was very uncharacteristic of him. "White walls, small beds, evil doctor ... not much else. He and other men took me when I was at the gorge. They covered my head and knocked me out."

He let go of me and groaned, throwing his head back.

"I told you the gorge was dangerous! That place is often patrolled. They're looking for me, remember?"

"Oh." I hadn't thought about that, and common sense should have kicked in. I couldn't blame Cole for that goof-up.

"What's done is done. Now we need to get you out of there. How long did you travel?"

I bit down on my lip. "I was apparently unconscious for four days before I woke up tied to a bed. So, there's no telling."

Cole puffed his cheeks and blew out air. "When I get you home, I'll have to babysit you constantly."

I glared at him, but he was most likely right. "The rashes have probably healed by now, so I'll be able to focus on how to get out."

"What rashes?" he asked cautiously.

"Wilson stuck me with a needle and had this silver flower extract infused into my veins. It wouldn't let me change and caused these burning, white spots."

"Midnight Nerium?"

"Yes, that's it." I looked at my skin where the rash had been.

"I think I know ... Nathalia?" Cole's eyes darted around as if he could no longer see me, even though I was standing right in front of him. Then he yelled, "I'm coming for you, don't do anything stupid!"

"It's working, see? There's movement in her muscles, just there."

"How long will it take the poison to leave her body?"

"About a day or so."

"We don't have that kind of time."

"Midnight Nerium is potent and thick. It moves slowly and there's nothing I can do to remove it faster."

I heard the two voices swirling above my head. At first, they were in the distance, then they were right in front of me.

"Your mad scientist game has already cost the Luminary thousands, Wilson. If you can't prove she has the canid powers in her blood within the week, they won't spend another dime on you."

I listened as the man gathered his things and walked from the room in expensive-sounding shoes. I cracked open my eyes to see Doc Wilson shaking his head while mixing liquids together. I focused on my surroundings. Cole and the lake were gone, replaced by medical supplies covering tables and catheter tubes on both my wrists. I tried to speak, but it came out a mumble because a smelly, rubber cup covered my mouth, like a muzzle.

"Ahh, you're awake. Good, that's good." He removed the cup so I could gasp in the air, not even a fraction as fresh as that of Vastaya's.

"You might feel ill at first. That's normal." Wilson continued clinking dishes and glass tubes together.

"None of this is normal!" I was sitting in a chair the length of a bed, with liquid tubes dripping into my veins.

"As I promised, no Midnight Nerium extract," he said after noticing me examining the bags.

"I heard you say it would take a while to leave my body. How long have I been asleep?"

"Weeks, my dear. Weeks. But I said no extract, I never said no *gas*."

I shot a look at the rubber cup that had just been around my mouth. I didn't tap into my astral body, I was all but forced into it. "You said I could help you."

Wilson turned to me. "And you did, Nathalia." He sat on a stool next to me, my arms and legs bound. "I am under a lot of pressure to succeed in my trials. You said you'd only been afflicted for a month. I thought it best to let you rest while I work on the solution."

"So, you kept me asleep?" I was mortified.

"Once your body is cleared, you will show me your fox form."

"I won't," I snapped, like a child refusing to eat their oatmeal.

Wilson's face fell into disappointment. "All your father did for the cause, even sacrificing his life, and yet his own daughter has succumbed to darkness and is unwilling to leave."

"My father?" I blinked.

"The Luminary has been searching for the Cold One for centuries. I am searching for the silver fox because I believe they are one in the same."

"And you think that's why they haven't found the Cold One … because they're looking for a person instead of an animal?"

"Precisely." Wilson picked up a syringe and extracted clear liquid from a tube.

I wasn't sure he'd tell me anymore – why would he care to explain anything to me? But I still dared to ask, "What's this about my father?"

"William and I joined the Luminary before he met your mother. We were compensated well. We were only boys when we heard the tales of the Cold One. We spent our time in the forest, searching for him, but never finding him. There's a reward for his capture. You can see how the money would attract a couple of young, poor boys. When we joined the Luminary, we dedicated all of our time into finding the devil. When William met your mother, he spent more time attending balls and parties. He missed official meetings more than once when you were born. He was nearly dismissed as a Luminary member, causing him to dedicate more time to his job."

The funding, that's where Father got his money. Probably why she married him, too.

"Still, we camped out at the gorge for days, year after year, waiting for the Cold One. The Feast Day was too dangerous for us to be there, but we hoped the Cold One would show himself on other days." He flicked the syringe. "When a boy of around eighteen walked into the clearing one evening, William didn't hesitate." Wilson pierced my skin with the needle as I protested, squirming and gritting my teeth as pain shot through my veins from where the needle had gone in.

But the doctor continued like he was doing a harmless routine procedure. "The boy mutated into a fox with long, silver fur." He pulled the needle out and pressed a piece of cloth to the injection site. "Your father slashed the animal's underbelly."

I stopped squirming.

"He didn't kill the fox," Wilson said, as if to ease my revulsion. "Instead, the Cold One ripped him to shreds. As I dragged my best friend's cold body from the dirt, I vowed to unmask the silver fox and put a stop to this madness."

I winced. Cole would never tear into a human because of a little scratch. He couldn't die, so what was the point of such retaliation unless it was pure rage? Cole was irritable, but not hateful.

I shook my head. "He wouldn't have."

Wilson's eyes hardened and lowered his voice. "There is no goodness in him, Nathalia. He is protecting them. His mother and her witch sisters."

I choked.

"You want to help me, don't you, Nathalia? I'm going to send the witches and their protector, the boy who killed your father," he added for effect, "back to Hell, but I need your instincts to find him."

I couldn't believe what I was hearing. It was too much, too confusing. I didn't know anything about my father, but I knew Cole. He was grumpy and sarcastic, but he wasn't a bad man. "I can't turn into a fox."

"Do not think me a simpleton, girl. I have done extensive studies on Midnight Nerium. It is the most potent type of Dogbane. Those white rashes told me all I need to know."

"*Anyone* could develop rashes after having a foreign substance drained directly into their bloodstream!" I argued, but he ignored me and I wondered if he'd tested the extract on innocent humans and animals to come to such a conclusion.

"There." He wiped his hands and tools. "Rest, now." Wilson disappeared, locking the door behind himself. He must have been flushing the poison from my body because I felt healthier. My mind, however, was consumed with the doctor's delightful little story. Mauling a human for no reason … I wondered if Wilson murdered my father and blamed it on Cole so he could get more money. He seemed greedy enough. And the son of a witch? Definitely not.

Cole knows how dangerous the Shkraykh are.

Wilson must have lied about it to get me to turn on him.

I had to find Cole, to tell him what Wilson had done, so I closed my eyes and focused on Vastaya. I couldn't clear my mind enough. Then it hit me … I didn't get there on my own the first time.

I turned my head and saw a syringe full of silver goo. I stretched my fingers over, just enough to roll the syringe onto my lap. I positioned it as best I could and jammed it into my leg, holding in a scream of anguish. I closed my eyes once again and envisioned the flowing wildflowers, so vibrant that no palette of paint could depict them properly.

I no longer felt pain, but the familiar kisses of dew drops on the grass. Vastaya's sweet smells lingered, welcoming me home.

Chapter Eleven
The Escape

"Cole?" I had been calling his name for hours, it seemed, trying to keep the elation of the astral world on the outskirts of my mind. I couldn't get lost again. "Cole! Where are you?"

Butterflies danced around my hair as I walked, beginning to lose hope of finding him, when I felt a touch. I turned and saw the white-blue eyes watching me. He opened his mouth to speak, but I flung my arms around his neck, pressing my cheek to his and breathing a sigh of relief. It took a moment for him to hug me back, but when he did, it was tight and loving, and I wanted to melt into him instead of facing what I had to say next.

"Wilson killed my father," I whispered.

His smooth face brushed mine as he pulled back, holding onto my waist and studying my face. "What?"

"My father." I bit down on my cheek and waited until the lump in my throat settled. "He was one of the hunters looking for you. Wilson told me he nicked the Cold One in the underbelly when he transformed into a silver fox, and that the fox tore into my father. Then Wilson said you're the son of one of the witches!" I rolled my eyes, keeping in the angry tears. "*He* took my father's life, so the Luminary would pay him more to catch the "dangerous" Cold One.

"Wilson didn't kill your father." He released me.

What it was about this realm, I didn't know, but Cole's delicate features invited me in. I moved a strand of hair from his forehead. "He did. He only said it so I'd hate you and turn you in. But I'd never do that."

"It was me."

"You'd never do something like that. You protect people. You're admirable."

He drew his brows in, like he was in pain, and gazed at me.

"Besides, you'd have some sort of nasty scar on your stomach if you—"

Cole removed his leather tunic and lifted the white shirt, revealing a part of his stomach where a pale-colored slash started at his naval and rounded the corner of his side. I stumbled back a step, feeling overcome by heat and dizziness.

"It's true." I clutched my stomach, Vastaya's air no longer refreshing but suffocating. "No wonder," I mumbled as I brought my eyes to his. "It makes sense. You never wanted to help me succeed. You refused to give me information, to teach me." I took a step closer, inches from his face. "You tricked the sprites, didn't you? And they *still* don't know, otherwise they'd put a stop to your madness." I turned to the wild fields. "Cole is protecting them!" I swung back to him and, with a hope that his words wouldn't be heart-shattering, I said, "Tell me I'm wrong. Tell me your mother isn't one of those creatures, and that Wilson *is* the reason I don't have a father." I couldn't hold back the tears now as they silently slipped down my cheeks.

He straightened and lifted his chin. "You're not wrong. I'm protecting my mother. And I defended myself when I was attacked."

I cried out, gritting my teeth, as I felt my physical body burning with the Midnight Nerium flowing through me.

"You can't die! You killed him for no reason," I wailed. "You took him from me. Now I'll never know if I could have been loved."

"It happened so quickly. I'd never been attacked by a human. It was self-defense, Nathalia. You know I would never purposefully kill —"

"I *don't* know that," I screamed, pulling at my hair, the affliction of the flower extract burning me.

"Stay, let me explain." He reached out.

I couldn't. The pain in my heart was tearing me away from the goodness of Vastaya. I screamed again, in anger, my heart throbbing with torment.

I felt every emotion rise from within as I ripped my

arms from their holds in Wilson's lab. I removed the syringe and tore the bags apart with my teeth.

"What in the … bring the sedation!" Wilson called as he swung open the door to witness me tossing a heavy metal tray clear across the room. I cast my wild gaze on the doctor, and with two swift movements, I jammed the flower extract syringe into his neck and picked him up, propelling his fat body into a shelf, toppling it and all the glass jars and bottles crashed on top of him.

I rushed from the room, manically growling like a beast. I couldn't transform until the poison left my bloodstream, but I was still strong enough to throw the two-hundred-pound man in a lab coat who tried to grab me, into the group behind him.

They threw themselves at me, trying to restrain the beast wreaking havoc and destroying the place entirely. But I was too strong, too fast. I tore from the facility to find myself in a garden blooming with silver flowers.

Midnight Nerium. My feet pounded on the ground as I ran past the flowers and through the thick trees of a surrounding forest, wishing I could disappear into my animal form and never return to the human Nathalia. At least then my heart couldn't be smashed into so many painful pieces.

As the moon grew in size, I knew I'd soon fall ill.

"A day or two left," I said, sitting alone near a small creek, washing my aching feet. Once the Midnight Nerium stopped burning my body, I'd spent a few days in fox form, hoping I'd eventually forget who I was. But I still cried in the night. I curled up in the grass and let the tears flow in confusion.

Why would the sprites allow him to protect the Shkraykh? I wanted to ask them, but I couldn't tap into the astral realm.

I should have grabbed some extract, I thought. I cleaned up my face and continued on my way, wondering how bad it would be to die.

I swatted at flies as I stepped through swamp water, hiking up my skirt so the smell wouldn't cling to the fabric. The air was dense and warm, though it was autumn, but I couldn't tell if my sudden faintness was from that or …

"No." I let out a single sob after scanning the darkening sky to see the moon, that cursed moon. Tonight was it for me. I could easily drop to the ground and let fate consume me. It'd certainly be easier than living out the rest of eternity with the one person who smashed any bit of trust I had in him. The one person I …

"Get a grip, Nathalia. It was Vastaya's influence," I said, almost feeling the warmth of Cole's cheek against mine again.

"Miss, what're you doin'?"

I jumped and spun around to see an older gentleman

with a hunting rifle in hand, crunching through the leaves.

"You look ill. Are ya ill, miss?"

More than you know. "I'm fine." I focused on his nose, trying not to let the world spin around me.

The man un-tied something from a satchel and handed me a canteen. I knew regular water wouldn't quench any thirst of mine, but I guzzled it down anyway. "Thank you, sir."

"Are ya lost?"

I chewed the side of my cheek, debating my answer. "Do you know the way to Moss Grove?"

"Why, it's only 'bout five miles that way." The kind man pointed me in the direction that would save my eternal life.

"What's your name, sir?"

"Henry. Henry Gardner, miss."

Knowing I was closer to the lake than I thought let my lungs breathe easier. "Thank you, Mr. Gardner."

As I walked down a small hill, I decided I'd start a journal of all the names of people who had been kind to me.

To keep my mind off the aches in my tired bones after another hour of moving, I thought about all the people I'd met who were worthy of my journal.

Mr. Gardner, Miss Burt – my schoolteacher, Tom from the general store, the inn owner who gave me a fresh rose after he heard Charlie call me a dimwit, Mrs. Nettle from down the lane who sometimes had me over for tea, my Pa – maybe, ... do the sprites count? The sprites, and Cole.

I shook my head after the last name unwillingly popped into my mind. When had Cole *ever* been nice to me?

He cares, a distant voice said, though I couldn't tell if it was my own thought or not. I ignored it, focusing on my throbbing feet. My stockings had gotten wet from the swamp and were rubbing against my boots, creating horrendous blisters and sores. I sat and pulled off the boots and stockings, wiggling my toes around in the cold grass.

It'd be easier if I were a fox. I brushed some hair from my face and went into my mind as I usually did to transform, but when I opened my eyes, I still sat with two legs in front of me. Again and again, I tried, but my fox form wouldn't come.

"What?" I said in a rather loud voice. I grumbled and pushed off the ground, leaving my boots and stockings behind. Pressure grew in my head and behind my eyes, and my stomach began writhing. I ripped off the top layer of my skirt, trying to cool off, but my body was like a stoked fire.

Crack an egg on me and it'll be cooked in a second. I stomped on, forcing myself to keep going. I didn't know if I was close to Gelid Lake, or had I taken a wrong turn? I stopped and rubbed my temples, wobbling slightly, then stumbled on, trying to get there as fast as my sick body would let me.

"Miss," an old voice called – a familiar one.

My muscles failed me, and I sank to my knees as I turned to face the man, like a person with no bones. "Mr. Gardner?"

I was hallucinating.

"Some water?" He offered his canteen again.

I lazily took it and put it to my lips as the trees blurred. Mr. Gardner's hands steadied me as I tipped the canteen back until water touched my lips. It was colder and smoother this time – perhaps because I was so tired and weak. I drank, and drank, and drank until the tree leaves were clear and blue in the full moonlight, and the bats' calls sounded in my ears. The crickets played a song, and the night frogs croaked in unison. I inhaled the crisp air, my lungs expanding to let it all in.

I wiped the side of my mouth with my thumb and handed the canteen back to Mr. Gardner.

"Once again, you've come to my rescue, sir." I smiled in thanks, feeling the blades of grass individually between my toes. It was then that I realized my feet didn't hurt, there were no sores. I lifted my long skirt to inspect, and sure enough, my smooth, pale skin was blemish free. I looked at my hands, then my arms – no wounds or cuts or bruises from Wilson. Then I directed my attention at Mr. Gardner, whose eyes were as white as the moon.

My shoulders dropped. "Cole."

The old man's features faded, his wrinkled jaw tightening, his scarce eyebrows filling in.

"I didn't think you'd talk to me," Cole said when he was put back together.

"And you were right." I didn't know what else to say.

"This is the —" he dramatically counted on his fingers, "fourth time I've saved you, and you *still* won't talk to me?" He was trying to make me laugh, but I didn't feel an ounce of joy.

"You," I began, ready to scream, to let all my anger unleash on him, but the words weren't there. "That was Gelid Lake water, I assume?" I nodded at the canteen I'd handed back. His smile faltered and he nodded. "Good. Then I'm all set for another month." I kept my throat tight so my voice didn't waver. His face was unreadable, which helped in this case. I could turn, walk home, and avoid him for the rest of the year. I'd be sure to make it to the lake in time next month. I'd camp out all day just to make sure he didn't get the chance to help me.

Cole touched my arm when I faced the woods leading to Moss Grove. "Your father," he began, "was the man who suggested plucking innocent men for the feeding."

I whirled around, not wanting to believe it. But I didn't know my father, not truly. I only knew who I wanted him to have been.

"I was always there when they forced the prisoners to walk the beam. I'd listen to the Luminary discuss what there was to be done. I'd watch from the woods as the Luminary's men wrapped the ropes around their necks and forced them onto the beam. They wanted the prisoners as fresh as possible for the Shkraykh, that's why they didn't hang them right away."

The words gagged me, and I saw Cole's hand reach for me out of the corner of my eye, but he retracted.

"Your father's words and actions ... I could see the fear in the innocents' eyes as they wobbled, crying and screaming, trying to balance on the beam. Well, they angered me. Years later, when he attacked me ..." He shook his head like he didn't want to continue.

Innocent people ... my father sentenced innocent people to a gruesome death. "But you took his life when you didn't need to," I countered, still not wanting to accept his words as truth.

"I told you, it was self-defense!"

"You can't die, Cole, did you forget that fact? And if you weren't protecting a coven of evil witches in the first place, you wouldn't have been put in that situation."

He took another step toward me. "My mother was good to me. I didn't know any better."

I inhaled his scent, the breeze gently washing it over me. "You can stop this." The feeling of my hope in him was overwhelming, even though he'd admitted to taking one of my parents away. "Accept that your mother was no good and find another cause to stand behind. Being immortal, you could do so much for the world."

His eyes blazed, and he backed away. "Just forget about her? Forget my own mother?"

"She did unspeakable things, Cole. Forget her and figure out how to destroy them for good."

He clearly took offense, and if I hadn't spent the last few months picturing the creatures mauling humans, I might find sympathy.

"What kills me, Cole," I said, feeling passion in my racing heart. "You told me those prisoners, the ones *you* deemed unworthy of a fair trial, deserved worse than the death they suffered. And yet you choose to protect a group of demons who are equally as guilty."

"If that's what you think of me, then maybe I deserve the same fate!" he snapped, clenching his jaw. I could see the defensive Cole arise – the one who thought of me as nothing but a little girl – a thistle.

I grew cold. "Maybe you do."

"You don't understand. You're still naive and probably won't grow out of that. Your goody-goody heart only sees black and white. You know what, Nathalia, you wouldn't be so brave if it weren't for me."

I narrowed my eyes, molten rage boiling through me. "You choose to protect someone who's done so much evil, caused so much fear, just because she's blood. The sprites took you in as their own, and gave you a beautiful gift, yet you still call that beast 'mother.' I can't condone that. I'm stronger than I was, Cole, and I can finally take control of what I want without questioning myself."

"You've come this far because of me. You grew up because of me. You'd still be climbing trees or crying in the mud if it weren't for *me*!"

"I'm done," I whispered, turning my back on him.

He scoffed. "You can't be done, Nathalia. You're an immortal guardian. You can't run away from your task, even if you can't understand its importance."

I rounded on him. "I mean I'm done with *you*, Cole. You can choose to keep the Shkraykh alive in their filthy home by yourself."

Cole blinked his white-blue eyes. "The sprites chose you —"

"And they're perfectly capable of choosing another for this wicked role. Goodbye, Cole." I left him standing there, slack-jawed.

I left *him*.

Chapter Twelve
The Last Moon

My paws beat against the frosty grass and my eyes focused on the tiniest details – birds fluffing their feathers in a nest, rodents jumping from naked branches. My ears twitched, homing in on sounds of prey – prey that I'd never need. My partly immortal body didn't need that type of nourishment. I never ate. I never slept. I never smiled.

It was almost Feast Day, but I refused to be a part of it. After my argument with Cole, I returned to Moss Grove, to my little cabin, and waited. I waited and avoided the north woods that led to the lake. I curled up in my little bed every night and pretended things were normal, desperately wishing I could escape into a dormant state and dream away this horrible life I'd been chosen for. I rarely traveled into town, not wanting the scornful questions the townspeople had for me.

I went to Gelid Lake once a month, opening all of my senses to detect if Cole was around. The water never moved and the sprites didn't whisper a sound. I knew they were disappointed in me, but I was in them, as well. So, I continued to heal my body, growing stronger with each month that passed. I could feel the pull to Vastaya grow the closer I came to immortality, but I resisted. I wanted no part in that life. Instead, I dreamed of a different purpose – helping the world in a way only one who couldn't die was able.

"My last night," I said, roaming the forest. The moon was bigger and brighter than ever that evening, as if the end of my human life were the grand finale – a great celebration.

I ran my fingers through the smooth glass water. *I could choose not to.* I hadn't felt an ounce of happiness since I'd left Cole and the sprites, and I often questioned if I ever could again.

"Please drink."

My heart dropped and the urge to flee hit me. I turned and saw Cole for the first time in eight months. He looked the same – of course – but his eyes were sad. For months, I wondered what I'd do or say when I saw him again, but now that he was standing in front of me, I was drawing a blank.

"Please," he said again.

"No." I could only say one word, worried if said more than that I'd break. I stood to leave.

"Nathalia," he said, pleading, blocking my way. He took my arm to stop me. I tried to jerk it away, but he didn't let me go. "I know you're hurt." When I stopped struggling, he dropped his hand. "I know you don't understand it, but I mourn my mother every day of my existence. The Feast Day is the only time I …" He growled, like he knew how abhorrent the words were when he said them out loud. "If I let go of that …"

"You'll mourn anyway. The creature that crawls from that grave is *not* her. It will never be her."

"You're just a naive little girl." His voice was barely a whisper and held no anger.

"Don't call me a little girl," I said, just as quiet.

I watched as his breathing quickened. He swallowed and our eyes met.

Oh my … My mind went blank as he lowered his face to mine, our lips only an inch from each other's.

My breathing hitched as my eyes flickered to his lips. I took a step back, regaining my senses as oxygen flooded my brain. I knelt beside the lake and scooped up some water, taking a long drink, savoring it, and contemplating if I should submerge myself and never come out. The moon brightened and the wind whistled. The sycamore danced as I was lifted from the ground, immersed in a brilliant light. I opened my arms to welcome the bliss, feeling happier and more at peace than I ever had – the only feeling I wanted to consume me.

The sprites danced in a circle around me, and I felt my heart stop, but it wasn't dead, as I thought it would be. Instead of beating, I felt it swirling with a pleasant tingle as if it had become the moon itself. I was lowered into the lake, its ripples glittering around me, spreading to the surface.

"Come," their voices sang. I opened my eyes to Vastaya, more vibrant and alluring than it had ever been.

"You're leaving us," the sprite said.

"I have to." Sadness saturated my voice and features as I struggled to hold back tears.

"Nathalia of the Trees, it has always been your decision."

Always been my decision? None of this had been my choice. It was a life I had been forced into. "Your wind pushed me into the lake! If I didn't come back every month, I'd be dead."

She smiled. "Go deep within your heart, child. Why did you climb our sycamore?"

Because I'm a tree-obsessed weirdo.

No, her voice replied in my mind.

"It called to me," I admitted, my newfound instincts and shimmering heart bringing awareness to me. "Like it was alive … like it wanted me to come *home.*"

"When you fell into the water, what happened?" another sprite inquired.

My head shot up, realizing my human self had forgotten the memory, but my immortal self remembered … I remembered.

Before they kissed me, securing my journey as an immortal, they gave me the option.

You will achieve great things, young one. You will effect a change in this world that will heal more hearts than one, they had said as I floated below the surface, and I had accepted.

"I can't do anything if I'm stuck here, letting those beasts exists just because —"

"Cole's heart is bigger than you think, Nathalia."

"Can't you stop him? You can't believe any of this is okay!" I began to work myself up. "Why *did* you give him immortality, anyway?"

"He pleaded for us to spare them when we were going to rid Vastaya of evil."

A third sprite spoke next. "We took in his plea and gave him the choice to be their guardian."

"Why did you let those things eat people?" I remembered the story about them crawling out and feeding on the towns.

"Sweet child," she said. "The decisions were placed in another's hands, and Cole learned quickly. The goodness in his heart was proven when he released all innocent prisoners."

"But he still let them eat other —"

"Monsters of the world," the first sprite said. "Cole kept them from roaming back into the world, preying on the innocent, just as he prevented the Shkraykh from doing the same."

I hadn't thought of it that way, but ... "And my father?"

"*We* love you, Nathalia."

I could feel the sprite's answer within me – my father wasn't good. He felt the same as my mother – I was a pebble in their leather-lined shoes.

"Now we are asking you to make your decision."

I stood, silent, for a long time as the sprites patiently waited. "Cole could just as easily take out the evil people, yet he relies on the Shkraykh to do it. It isn't right."

"The choice to stop is his."

"He made it clear he won't stop." The sprites frowned. They knew my answer before I said it. "I can't stay."

The illumination enhanced, blanketing me in brilliant white light, as they bowed their heads, then faded as they left me at the lake's edge, standing in front of Cole.

The hope in his eyes killed me.

"How do you feel? Anything like a rose, yet?" he joked with a side smirk.

"I'm sorry," I said, refusing to return his smile. His face fell, and my heart broke. "I can't be part of this." I brushed past him, our hands swiftly touching, like a final goodbye.

Chapter Thirteen
Still a Thistle

Sometimes I wish I'd drowned when I fell from the great sycamore. I wish my mother *had* sent me to that hospital in Harburgh where I could successfully lose myself – my mind … my heart. My birthday came and went three times. So did the Feast Day. I didn't acknowledge either.

Instead, I traveled, lending a hand where and when I could – anything to take my mind off thoughts of ice-blue eyes and ash hair, sweet-smelling moss, and healing waters.

I let a single tear slide down my cheek as I sat in a wrought-iron chair. Time didn't seem to exist for me.

Three years, I thought, feeling like it'd only been yesterday I left Cole and the sprites. I rubbed my reddened nose and looked over the balcony my chair was on – the Eiffel tower sat mere miles away. My mindless roaming had brought me to France where I found a missionary for parentless children. Orphans. Like me.

"Nathalia? What are you doing out here on such a chilly evening?" Caroline, the head of the missionary, wrapped a shawl around my shoulders, covering the silk sleeves that ran down to my elbows. The dress Cole had gifted me – I never got rid of it. I tried to donate it more than once, but I couldn't part with it.

"Just thinking." I sighed, admiring the rhinestone sky.

"About the children, again?"

I nodded.

"Do you not see how happy they are?"

I turned to her. "But they have no home!"

Caroline looked around dramatically. "What would you call this, then?" She cracked a smile. "You must not torture yourself for not being able to give every child what you think they deserve."

I clenched my jaw. I had eternity to achieve that very goal.

I felt a palm rest on my fidgeting hands. "They have a family with us."

I met Caroline's kind, wrinkled eyes.

"You don't need a mother and father to be part of a family. You just need love."

I blinked away tears.

"And they're not as unhappy as you think they are." She swiped a gray curl from her forehead. "Children are innocence, itself. They can see things we can't and appreciate the smallest of things."

"Like what?" I pulled the wool shawl tight as a gust of wind blew past us.

"They see the magic in fireflies, and the wishes on stars. When it rains, they don't shiver from the cold and wish the sun would come out. They splash in the puddles and dance under the clouds. Children find goodness, even in the most wanting of times."

I grinned. Caroline put it into such a beautiful perspective.

"They're lucky to have you," I said.

"They're lucky to have us both." She kissed my head and went inside.

I gazed back at the sky and imagined a shooting star flying past me. What would I wish for? I scanned Earth's navy-blue dome, but all I could see was the moon peeking out from behind a small cloud. I knew the third Feast Day since I'd changed had come. It was a day of agony for me, knowing Cole was out there grieving his mother as I grieved for my parents. I mourned the lack of morality none of them ever held. But I chose to move on, unlike Cole. He —

Nathalia.

My heart quickened. I knew who whispered to me. I squeezed my eyes shut and gulped down the glass of chardonnay in front of me.

Nathalia, they said in unison. I pulled the shawl over my head and pressed my forehead to my knees.

Again, they called, the urgency in their heavenly voices pulling at me. My fear dried up as I realized I was needed. I stood and walked to the edge of the balcony.

The moon smiled down, and in the glowing haze surrounding it, I thought I saw the sprites dancing. I gripped the iron rail and focused on the light.

It burnished and became pearlescent, and I knew where I was: Vastaya.

"Our child, you have returned." The sprites surrounded me, and a smile pulled at my lips. The warm welcome soaked into me, and I wondered why I ever stayed away.

"Cole needs you," one sang.

My head hung. "I've already told you my decision, I —"

"He is your family, Nathalia."

My lips parted as the word hung in the air. These beings, pure and good, loved Cole. They saw him as good-natured and not a lost cause as I treated him. And Caroline? She was right ... a mother and father didn't make a family. Love did.

"We chose you, Nathalia. You're good for him."

I remembered them saying the same thing three years ago, but I could never understand what they meant.

"You know what it feels like to have parents who chose unsavory paths." The more the sprites spoke, the more I wanted to kick myself for being so stupid, for being cold-hearted. The fact that I'd lived willingly with the pain my parents caused made me a hypocrite. I'd held onto their memory just as Cole held onto his mother's.

"He needs you, now."

Still, I hesitated. I knew it wasn't fair, but he had made his choice. The sprite's ecru eyes squinted, only slightly, as if she knew I'd make the right decision.

But could I? Love makes a family – a certain type of love. A deep, caring, sometimes heartbreaking love; one that can never be forgotten. A love that protects, comforts, laughs, and sometimes fights.

The sprites blurred like flickering candle lights standing about, causing a serene, calming place for my mind to wander. And it did. I could almost feel the frost of the winter, the lonely nights counting the falling snowflakes.

Snow … Cole's eyes. His face, his smooth skin and soft hair, and the eyes that had shown me emotions I didn't realize he had felt until just then. His concern when I had nearly fallen into the gorge before I was immortal, and the sadness when I told him I was nothing to my mother. Then the vividness of his image brightened, showing me his face the day I left.

Heartbreak. Tears welled in my eyes as I stomped the ground in frustration. I loved him. I loved him so desperately I felt like the air was sucked from my lungs. An immortal can't die from suffocation, but at that moment, I swear I could have perished if I didn't feel his arms wrapped around me soon.

I'd made my decision. If the only way Cole could cope with the loss of his mother was by seeing her once a year, even as a demonic creature, then I would fight by his side for all eternity.

"He has chosen," the silky voice said.

I glanced around to see the sprites in their full forms; with dark-golden skin and sheen dresses, all watching me. Cole wanted to stop – to end the suffering of so many.

I could barely speak, but they knew, even before I did, what my answer was. Their warm smiles were love itself. They motioned to the lake, and as I stepped in, the world grew dark. Marred screams filled the night – a battle cry of hate, desperation, and loss of hope. The heartbreak of a son losing his mother once and for all.

I leaped into action, shrinking into fur-form within seconds, as if the past three years hadn't happened and I'd never left the lake, and dove deep into the water. I didn't need to breathe – my speed was so great not even a fish could outswim me. I burst from the water like a silver bullet through the woods, faster and faster as the shrill voices pierced my pointy ears.

The group of women-like creatures in tattered, black gowns caught my attention first, then a circle made of candles and symbols. Then —

COLE.

I sprang into human form as I ran and jumped from the ledge to the gorge floor, briefly thanking my immortal body for not fracturing with impact. My adrenaline pumped furiously as I watched the Shkraykh sink their filthy teeth into Cole's arm. The second my bare feet hit the dirt, I took off, barreling into one of the witches and sending her smashing into the rock wall on the other side of the escarpment. I snagged one by the hair and whipped her into another. Now their attention was on me.

Good.

Cole's eyes were colossal at my appearance, like he was wondering if I was really there, or perhaps just in shock that I was. Without hesitation, I pulled him up by the arm and pushed him out of the way as the pack of Shkraykh began to circle me like hungry wolves. Their chattering laughter disgusted me, but I used the repulsion to fuel me. I jumped and twirled, kicking them hard enough to knock a head off, but they didn't perish.

"The circle," Cole called in a weak voice.

I clutched a Shkraykh by the shoulders and tossed her directly into the ring of candles. With a horrendous cry, she burst into ash, momentarily shocking me – just long enough for thousands of knives to latch onto my arm. With a roar, I tore the nasty beast off by her hair, fending off another whose mouth came too close to my face. One bit my shoulder, and I cried out, trying to wrap my arm around her neck to release her forceful grip.

She was suddenly yanked back, and I turned to see the silver fox. I, too, morphed, and together, Cole and I bounced between fox to human like bolts of sharp lightning, fighting in both forms. I threw another witch to the mercy of the circle, ashes consuming her. Another went flying and sizzling. One by one, we destroyed them, sending them to the pits of Hell where they belonged.

I dared smile at our success, a short-lived burst of joy, when I saw the last one crouched over Cole's human body, feeding on him. Passion of every form coursed through me, shaking my bones and nearly blinding me as I darted over to them.

"He's mine." I had a fire in my voice and fireworks in my heart as I clutched her neck, lifting her into the air, not caring when her snake-like tongue shot out at me or that her dirty, yellow nails clawed at my arm. I didn't care that her hollow, coal-black eyes devoured me, burning through my soul. I took her to that circle and stared at her face, my intuition flashing within me. This was Cole's mother. I turned my head to him, ignoring the blood dripping from where she was digging into my skin.

Cole was on his knees, watching, bloodied and bruised, an aching sadness written across his face, darkening his usually bright eyes. This is what she had done to him – she caused this. I looked back at the snarling beast in front of me.

"You'll never hurt him again." I threw her into the circle and watched the ashes spark and snap, consuming her. I clenched my jaw and my nostrils flared as the witch joined her sisters below.

127

Silence fell, and I ran to Cole, gently wrapping my arms around him, brushing the hair from his face and pressing my forehead against his.

"You're dying, aren't you?" I whispered, and he choked out a laugh.

"I can't die in any mortal way, but the Shkraykh —" He coughed up blood. "They have venom."

I dragged my thumb over his lip, wiping off the blood.

"Every year I make it to the lake to heal, but this year ... I've never battled them all head-on at once. I've never been the target."

I supported his weight, preparing to help him to the lake, but as I looked up from the bottom of the gorge, he said, "Hopeless."

"No, no." I desperately surveyed the place. I knew I could climb out, but not while carrying him. "Sprites," I called. "Please help!"

"They can't, Nathalia. They're bound to the lake. The curse did that."

I screamed out in frustration. "What can I do?"

My knees buckled as he collapsed. He struggled to breathe as he laid his head in my lap. I closed my tear-filled eyes as his hand caressed my cheek.

"We don't have to worry about them anymore," he said with a small, wheezing breath.

I inhaled and looked into his eyes. "After all these years, what made you change your mind?" I pressed his hand to my face, savoring its warmth against my skin.

"I think you know."

I cried and pulled him close, rocking him and sobbing into his hair.

He touched the silk of my now-tattered sleeve. "You're wearing the dress."

I could only let out a disgusting snort-cry.

"Nathalia," he whispered, his voice strained.

"Cole," I blubbered, wondering if this was it – the moment he'd go forever.

"You're squishing me."

I nearly dropped him as I relaxed my grip, not wanting to cause more pain, but his smile and weak laugh showed me he was still himself ... still that sarcastic Cole.

"The canteen." He pointed to a scrawny tree where his leather canteen hung. I gently laid his head on the ground and then ran to fetch it.

"Do I pour it on your wounds?"

He shook his head as best he could and took it from my hands. I thought he was going to drink it as he unscrewed the cap, but he reached out and began pouring it down my arm.

I snatched it from his hands. "No!"

His raspy breathing worsened. "Let me."

I watched as the multiple claw marks healed before my eyes, leaving only white scars, and immediately poured the rest of the water on Cole's deepest wounds, ignoring his pleas of, "Don't."

"Mine aren't as bad as yours." I pushed his hand away and kept pouring.

"Exactly. You can heal and go on."

I shook my head rapidly. "You wouldn't be in this mess if I had been here. I don't know why the sprites thought I could do anything. All I've done is disappoint you."

"Do you truly not know why the sprites chose you?" Cole's voice held a certain exasperation, like I couldn't see something right in front of me.

"It's not hard to choose someone who's so easily discarded." I remembered the pain my mother's words and coldness toward me caused, and it became almost unbearable as I watched Cole suffer.

His knuckles brushed my cheek. "You won't be discarded by your true family."

Tears flooded my eyes. Cole was my true family, even on his grumpiest of days, he had been there to help me – to keep me alive. I pressed my lips to his cheek and told him to hold on, to be strong, then I ascended the cliff at high speed to fill the canteen again, ignoring his protests.

I attempted to morph to move faster, but it didn't work. The Shkraykh had some type of debilitating venom, one that prevented my transformation … one that would kill us. It had finally hit my bloodstream, I could feel it. I ran as fast as I could and jumped into the water, dunking the canteen in. I knew my cuts and abrasions would heal in the water, but it would take some time for the venom to leave my bloodstream. I was stuck in human form for a while.

"I'm coming," I called to him as the cliffs came back into view.

"You okay?" My voice echoed through the canyon.

"Peachy." He clutched his side with shaky hands and tried to sit up. I licked my lips, knowing I was too weak to cascade down the cliffs as I had done before. As I moved to descend to a ledge, my arm was grabbed from behind. I spun around to see an old, hairy face with bad breath glaring down at me.

"Doc Wilson," I gasped, wondering how he survived through my fit of rage back in his lab those years ago.

"Thought you could best me, Cold One?"

"You don't have to do this. We defeated the Shkraykh – they're gone."

He cackled mockingly. "And why would I believe you?" He peered down and noticed Cole, and I could see on his face that he knew Cole was dying. His sneer made me want to punch him, to rip his teeth out and make him swallow them.

"What's in the canteen?"

"Water," I replied, not knowing if he knew about Gelid Lake's healing waters. Either way, he wasn't going to let me help Cole.

"Let's go." Wilson pulled me away from the edge, but

I wasn't going down without a fight. I tossed the canteen over the cliff's edge, hoping it would land near Cole, and I kicked Wilson in the kneecap. He howled but whipped his hand across my face. The slap knocked me off my feet, stunning me. I jumped up, but a sharp burn in my stomach disabled me. I dropped to my knees and saw a silver dagger lodged into me, my blood cascading around it, staining my dress a deep crimson.

"Infused with the most potent Midnight Nerium." The doctor lifted his chin, proud of his cheap shot. I gripped the hilt, gasping for air.

He knelt, coming close to my face. "You and your demon mate have ruined my reputation for the last time." He backed away. "After your little escape, the Luminary pulled the funding. They said there was a lack of proof, even after you tore apart my lab and injured several full-grown men, but I'll finally be able to hand you over. You've been hiding for quite some time, haven't you, Monster?" He smirked as I tried to pull the knife out, but the pain was too much and I screamed out.

"Strong, isn't it?" He chuckled as I began to pant. "I spent the last few years developing the richest form of extract I could, hoping to meet you here one day."

"Your vendetta against us is in vain, you malignant piece of trash," I spat, trying not to vomit.

Wilson gripped the hilt of the dagger, pushing it in deeper.

"Get ... away from ... her." Cole was climbing over

the cliff's edge, breathing through each word.

"Not dead yet? That's fine. You can watch as I drain this demon of life, then you'll be next."

My world was fading, my vision becoming a dark blur, but not before I felt the dagger being ripped from my stomach and saw Cole jam it into the side of Wilson's neck. The man's eyes bulged, and he crashed backward, flailing as he died.

Cole wrapped his arm around my waist, but it was too late. He disappeared from sight and I was taken far away from him.

I had just gotten him back, but I was destined to be alone.

"Wake, my child."

"Sprite?" I inhaled and opened my eyes. "I'm dead."

"You have been sleeping for a while, but you are not dead." The sprite knelt by my side.

I sat up at the edge of Gelid Lake.

"You have restored Vastaya."

"But something feels different. I—"

"You are not in the astral realm, but you are not on Earth, either. Vastaya is once again a safe haven, one that no mortal can enter. You sacrificed your Earthly body by casting out the Shkraykh, and it has given us back our home."

"We truly are immortal, then?"

She smiled and bowed her head in confirmation.

"Nathalia?"

I whipped around to see Cole strutting toward me. No bite marks or scratches, no strained breathing. The smirk across his face told me he knew he'd end up here. I leaped up and got right in his face. "You let me embarrass myself back there, crying with snot running down my nose when you *knew* we wouldn't really die!" I'd started replaying the pathetic scene over in my mind, probably more dramatic than it had been, but it haunted me.

He stifled a grin. "It was sweet to see how much you cared."

I took a deep breath, trying to calm myself at his sardonic tone.

"Technically our Earth bodies died, so —"

I poked him in the chest. "You are *so* annoying!"

"Yeah, but you like it."

I growled in frustration and crossed my arms. "How do you gather that?"

"Would you have kissed me otherwise?"

I felt my cheeks burn, and I tried to form a coherent sentence. "I, you … you were dying! And it was only on the cheek. Oh, wipe the grin off your face, Cole."

He sucked his teeth, looked at the sky, then back at me with his brows raised and a smile pulling at the side of his mouth.

I kept my face relaxed, trying not to fall into his entrapping gaze.

"You wanna go for a swim?"

"No!" I knew I was being ridiculous, my anger only induced by the sheer humiliation of kissing him on the cheek and obnoxiously wailing in his ear.

"How long are you going to throw your temper tantrum?" He examined his wrist as if looking at a watch. "I might have time for a nap."

I glared at him, arms still crossed.

"Would it help if I embarrass myself?"

I furrowed my brow, wondering what he meant.

My shimmering heart skipped a chime as he closed the gap between us and caressed my cheek with his fingertips. My arms dropped in shock as his lips brushed mine. I stood there, limp, thinking of nothing but his hands and mouth.

He pulled away, still holding my face, and looked into my eyes. "Satisfied?"

Most definitely.

"Can we go swimming now?"

What happened next wasn't the influence of Vastaya, but my own desires. I jumped into his arms and kissed him. He supported my weight, holding me as close as he could, kissing me back.

His hands moved to my waist and squeezed my hips.

Then Cole catapulted me into the lake, following close behind. We both surfaced, and I wiped my eyes and splashed him.

"*Cole*," I chided.

"*Nuh-tahl-yuh*," he mimicked, then pulled me to him.

"Does this mean I'm a rose?" I smirked, wrapping my arms around his neck.

"Nah, you're still a thistle."

I pushed him away. "Excuse me?"

"I don't want a rose." Cole's face sobered as he bobbed in the water.

"You still think I'm rabbit food, after all this time? After everything?"

He breathed a laugh through his nose. "Have you ever seen a thistle, Nathalia? Their spines are made of spikes, but their blooms are vibrant and full of nutrients. Roses are pretty, and their thorns are sharp, but I would choose the weed every time."

"The weed, huh?" I couldn't hide the disappointment in my voice. I wanted to be a rose to him.

"Do you truly not know how beautiful you are, Nathalia? Inside and out?" He leered at me.

I treaded water, my mouth parting at the intensity in his voice.

He swam forward, taking my hands in his and pressing them to his lips. "You're my gorgeous thistle, and I love you."

We heard the harmonious rejoice of the sprites, and I caught a glimpse of my reflection in the water. I remember when the sprites told me I was different in

Vastaya, but I couldn't see it before. Now, examining myself, I could. My eyes – not a different color, but a different emotion. I had finally let go of the hurt. I wasn't discarded. I was found. Cole's reflection appeared next to me and I rested my head on his shoulder, admiring the two of us, finally where we were meant to be.

· ——⚙— ·

Cole and I stayed in the water for hours, though mortal time didn't exist in Vastaya. I squeezed the water out of my hair and skirts, not able to wipe away the mirth painted on my face as I watched him run fingers through his hair.

"What?" He'd noticed me staring.

"I'm sorry I took so long." I bit the inside of my cheek and fidgeted with my hands until Cole took them in his.

"Do you know what a few years is like for an immortal?"

My eyebrows turned up, questioning his meaning.

"It's like I only had to wait a few minutes for you." He let go of my hands and patted my head. "You're still little, but you'll understand one day."

I tackled him, pinning him to the ground. *"Don't* call me little."

"So, you no longer feel weird about me being two hundred years old?"

"Correction – eighteen for two hundred years." I

137

pressed my hands to his cheeks and kissed him, the elation we both felt making us giggle, knowing we'd never know loneliness again.

"Children." The sprites stood before us as we jumped up, holding in snickers as if we were forbidden sweethearts caught by our parents.

"You have proven to us that your hearts are true and good."

Cole and I eyed each other with admiration, then looked back to the sprites.

"As always, we will give you a choice for your future. You may stay with us in Vastaya forever or return to Earth."

I didn't want to leave, and why would I? Everyone who loved me was within the walls of these most precious lands.

"Mothers," Cole addressed them in a professional tone. "If we choose to leave, will we be able to see you again?"

Their charming laughter flowed around us. "Oh, son. Vastaya will always be open to you."

I met his eyes, sparkling from his handsome smile.

"But," a sprite said. "Your mortal bodies are forever gone on Earth. You will enter the world as spirits."

The disappointment I felt dragged me down. As a "human" immortal I had so much to give. What could I do as a spirit?

Happiness, daughter, they whispered.

Cole's arm wrapped around my waist.

I brought my eyes to their brilliant lights and smiled. My family was around me, hugging me and kissing me, and I finally saw the small miracles in the world.

Chapter Fourteen
All the Small Things

Cole and I have been around for a long time, but you've never seen us the way we look within the realm of Vastaya. We no longer have the ability to save the world as I'd once hoped we could, but we still found a way to bring happiness.

Sometimes, if you look closely enough, you can see us dancing – in the shadows of falling snowflakes, or on the tail of a shooting star. Cole kisses me when the ocean waves crash, and the fresh spring breeze blows. Our laughter drifts upon fluffy dandelion seeds, and our songs can be heard in a child's giggle.

We can't stop you from falling and scraping your knee, and we don't have the capability to heal a broken heart, but we will bring you signs of love and goodness. Listen with your heart and feel our kisses upon your cheeks.

When you feel the loneliness consume you, let the smells of nature envelope your senses. Listen to the wind rustling through the trees. Feel the sun and moon caress your skin. Dig your bare toes into the Earth, and dance to the songs of the birds. Taste the air that fills your lungs and gives you life, and never forget how significant you are to us – to the sprites, and to the world.

Cole and I will share our happiness with you – live it through you, for our love is endless, and we will be your family forever.

Epilogue

"You have twigs in your hair. What'd you do, run through a beaver dam?"

"Shut up," I said to Cole, pulling out the tiny sticks from my tangled locks. We had just changed back from foxes to our astral bodies. I'd always been grateful to the sprites for letting us keep our fox forms in Vastaya.

I felt Cole's fingers running through my hair, sending shivers down my arms.

"It's almost all silver, now," he whispered in my ear. It was true – my hair was *finally* turning as ash-blond as Cole's. And I loved it.

I turned to him and brushed his cheek with the back of my hand. He wrapped his fingers around my hand and kissed my palm. "I have something for you." He weaved his fingers through mine and pulled me along until we were at the base of the great sycamore, overlooking the beautiful, heavenly Gelid Lake that gave me my purpose, my life - my everything. A small pile of something caught my eye below.

"Wanna skip rocks?" Cole asked, releasing my hand

and grabbing up a flat rock from the foot-high pile of perfectly smooth, oval stones.

"Did you collect these?"

"No, Nathalia. I had the squirrels do it."

I grinned and took a stone. On the count of three, we both tossed the rocks at the water. Cole won.

"Again," I said. Again and again and again, and still, his stone skipped the surface more than mine.

I was determined to beat him, otherwise, his gorgeous, presumptuous smirk would last for the rest of the night. I snatched the next stone, but as I brought it up, I hesitated. This particular stone had a painting depicted on it ... one that sucked the breath from my immortal lungs.

"I'm no artist, but I tried." Cole was behind me as I stared at the rock in my hands. A blotchy scene of an ash-haired boy with an outstretched arm was holding a bouquet, and a girl was receiving them. The bouquet in his hands?

"Thistles," I whispered.

"Happy birthday, Nathalia." Cole kissed my forehead and held me close. I closed my eyes, feeling his lips on my cheek as he enveloped me in his warm, strong hold. I had forgotten my birthday once. For seventeen years my age was forgotten by people who were supposed to love me. Now, I felt more love than I could have ever imagined, to the point where I forgot my *own* birthday.

Cole, however, has never missed one, even after the one hundred and twenty-four years we've been together.

"I love you."

ABOUT THE AUTHOR

V. Mull, born in 1991, found a love for writing at a young age. She often finds inspiration for her many stories within Maine's beautiful woods where she lives with her husband, three children, and their pets.

She pens a few different genres such as Young Adult Fantasy, Horror, and Children's Stories.

In 2019 her short story, *The Queen and the Pebble* won first place in Pixie Forest Publishing's Summer contest. Her name also lies in print in *Phobia! An Anthology of Fear*, *Cozy Kisses* - A romantic anthology, her novella, *The Feared*, and debut novel, *The Seven Lands of Cador: Storm of the Elements*.

Mull's greatest wish is to create worlds into which people can escape, and will work hard to make this dream come true.

Liked this book?
Please leave a review!

Reviews are important to authors and publishers. Please take a moment to leave a review on Amazon and/or Goodreads.

They help authors sell more books.

20-25 reviews and Amazon includes the book in the "Also Bought" and "You Might Like" lists.
50-70 reviews and Amazon highlights the book in spotlight positions and in its newsletter.

Thank you!

www.ingramcontent.com/pod-product-compliance
Lightning Source LLC
Chambersburg PA
CBHW060834120626
46557CB00001B/492